A PEBBLE
AND A PEN

A Pebble and a Pen

Joan Donaldson

Holiday House / New York

Thank you to Joseph Pucci,
Professor of Classics at Brown University,
for reviewing the Latin translations

penmanship on jacket, title page,
and pages *x*, 27, 40, 41, 49, 111, 131, 139, 144 © by Michael R. Sull
penmanship on pages 39, 56, 116, 140, 145 © by Joan Donaldson

Library of Congress Cataloging-in-Publication Data
Donaldson, Joan.
A pebble and a pen / Joan Donaldson.—1st ed.
p.   cm.
Summary: In 1853, fourteen-year-old Matty runs away from the drudgery of farm life
to join Mr. Spencer's famous penmanship school and finds she must meet many
challenges to make her way as a female penman.
ISBN 0-8234-1500-7
[1. Penmanship—Fiction. 2. Sex role—Fiction. 3. Spencer, Platt R. (Platt Rogers),
1800–1864—Fiction] I. Title.

PZ7.D714985 Pe 2000
[Fic]—dc21   00-021777

ACKNOWLEDGMENTS

With a grateful heart
I thank the following people for their help
in creating this story.
Debbie and Michael Sull, my teacher and Master Penman
Ellen Howard, my mentor
Regina Griffin, my editor
The Fire Keepers, my beloved critique group
composed of Deborah Fisher, Tracy Groot,
Betsy Kaylor, and Karmen Kooyers
Katie Kooyers, for her photographic skills
Marie C. Bolchazy, for permission to quote
the Latin phrases found in Bolchazy-Carducii's
Artes Latinae course
Linda Otto Lipsett, for allowing me
to copy a motto from *Remember Me*
My family, John, Matthew, and Carlos
And above all, thanks be
to God.

For John, a Master Farmer,
and Karmen Kooyers,
my *amica certa*

Origin of Spencerian Writing

Evolved mid nature's unpruned scenes,
  On Erie's wild and woody shore,
The rolling wave, the dancing stream,
  The wild rose haunts—in days of yore.

The opal, quartz, and ammonite,
  Gleaming beneath the wavelet's flow,
Each gave its lesson—how to write—
  In the loved years of long ago.

I seized the forms I loved so well,
  Compound them as meaning signs,
And to the music of the swell,
  Blent them with undulating vines,

Thanks, nature, for the impress pure!
  Those tracings in the sand are gone;
But while the love of thee endures,
  Their grace and ease shall still love on.

Platt Rogers Spencer (1800–1864)

VIRTUTE et LABORE

THIS

IS AWARDED TO

Matilda Anne Harris

for satisfactory completion of the prescribed course of study in the Eighth Grade at the Manlius Common School.

Signed: *Harvey Nettleton*

May 24, 1853

Manlius, Michigan

CHAPTER

I

Matty positioned her eighth-grade certificate in the sunlight that filtered through the tall pines surrounding the log cabin. The loft where she stood was stuffy and smelled of the onions swaying over her head. She shoved back the fraying cuffs of her dress and for the sixth time that day read aloud her new certificate.

"*Virtute et Labore*. Awarded to Matilda Anne Harris, signed Mr. Harvey Nettleton, Manlius, Michigan, on May 24, 1853." Mr. Nettleton had flourished the Latin motto, and the letters of his signature swooped across the diploma like swallows. If only she could write so beautifully! She would have to labor hard to match his skills. But when she had them, she would live in some far-off city and escape all the weeding, washing, and cooking that gave her no time to read or write.

Did she dare snatch a few moments of daylight to practice and risk her mother's ire? Propping the certificate against the wall, Matty settled herself at the table her brother Abe had built for her. She opened her copybook, laid it in front of her, dipped her quill, and froze. Someone was climbing the ladder to the loft.

"Matilda!" her mother's scratchy voice rose into the loft. "Drat the wretched girl!"

There was no place to hide. Matty held her breath.

Her mother gripped Matty's shoulder and pulled her around. "I walk away, and you're back to your fool letters. Why aren't you down tending to supper?"

Matty focused on a knothole in the floor by her toes. "The soup's done, and the boys aren't in from the fields yet. I thought I might practice a bit, seeing that I churned and baked all afternoon. I even carried in extra water. It *is* my graduation day."

Her mother picked up the diploma. "I must have been daft to agree when Abe pleaded to let you graduate. Little good my own diploma ever did me. Just led me to marry a useless scholar who didn't even know which end of the plow to hitch up." She stared at the diploma again and then tossed it aside. "Ben Cooper's proposal will prosper you more. Every acre of his farm is paid for, and he bought the lumber for a clapboard house."

Matty sucked in her breath. "Ma, I don't want to marry Ben." Ben with his greasy hair and bony fingers would never lay a hand on her! "All he wants is a woman to care for his seven children," she mumbled.

"The foolishness of youth. You'd never be wanting with Ben." Her mother shook her head. "Enough of this scribbling! Go mind the kettles."

Matty could sense her mother's disapproval as she descended the ladder. All her ma could think about was cooking and babies. There'd be no use telling her about Mr. Nettleton's offer to recommend Matty for Mr. Spencer's business seminary. Ma would never say yes.

Matty stirred the kettle and watched her mother give Teddy his supper. He grabbed for the spoon, and Ma crooned baby talk as he scooped up mush. Gently she cleaned the toddler's chin with her apron, and her eyes were calm when she glanced up at Matty.

"Ma . . ." Matty began. She jerked the spoon rapidly through the pot, and beans tumbled into the fire. "Mr. Nettleton would like to send me East to a business school."

"Mind the beans! Hopeless, just hopeless," her mother moaned. "Who does that schoolmaster think he is, putting such notions into your head? You've more learning now than you'll ever need. You best be learning more womanly skills. If it's a trade you're after, you can study midwifery with me."

"But, Ma, I've no talent for nursing. The sight of blood turns my stomach. I want to be a penman. They make good money."

"Matilda, there is only one place for a woman, minding a home and caring for children." Her mother smiled at the herd of boys tumbling through the doorway. "You'll understand when you have your own. No decent woman works at a business."

Twelve-year-old Tom snorted. "That's all Matty talks about. 'If only I could be a penman.'"

The guffaws of her brothers beat against her like hail. Matty hurried to fill the bowls, and one of her braids fell into the kettle, sloshing soup over the edge.

Her mother groaned. "Not so hasty, Matilda! When will you ever be careful?"

Matty's older brother, Abe, smiled at her. His cambric shirt, streaked with sweat, clung to his broad shoulders. Abe was like one of his oxen, steady and calm.

"But I thought only men were penmen," Abe said. "Aren't women too delicate for business?"

"Mr. Spencer's daughter Sara can write a fine hand," Matty said. "She even teaches with her pa."

"Who's she?" Tom asked, reaching over the plank table for a chunk of bread.

"The daughter of America's greatest penman, Platt Rogers Spencer." Matty waved the ladle in the air, nearly hitting Abe. "Please let me go, Ma! Mr. Nettleton thinks I have the ability to be a good copier."

"Cease prattling about Mr. Spencer, Matilda. I promised Mrs. Chapman that you'd go to her cabin on Monday. Helping out during the last weeks of her confinement will be more suitable for you."

In her mind Matty could hear Mr. Nettleton telling her, "With your determination and common sense

4

you should study penmanship. You could work in the business world as a clerk." Those skills could liberate her from the snares of wedlock and house-keeping. She certainly wasn't seeking more clothes to scrub.

"Is somebody coming?" Abe asked.

Matty jumped up and opened the door. Ben Cooper's wagon rumbled into the clearing. He halted his team, and children spilled out of the wagon like foam off a kettle of bubbling jam. Matty's brothers raced out to Ben's boys while Sally, the six-year-old girl, tried to manage the youngest.

Matty took a step back. Not Ben Cooper! Having those two sets of twins had probably killed his wife, she thought. If only there was a back door she could slip out of. But it was no use. The whole lot of Coopers moved toward her cabin like a swarm of bees searching for a new hive.

"Matilda, where are your manners!" Mrs. Harris scolded and bustled up behind her. "Here, fetch in those young'uns." Her mother pushed her out the door. "Move along now."

Quickly the children engulfed Matty, and Sally handed her the two babies. "Pa says you're gonna be our new ma!" one twin chattered.

"Is it true, Miss Matty?" his twin asked. He twirled around, and one of his arms hit his younger sister.

The two-year-old began to howl.

"Hush," Sally said. She looked up at Matty.

Matty paled. Just the laundry for this horde would take all week to wash. Not to mention all the mending, sewing, and preserving. A body would never have time to read.

"You're right pretty like that, Miss Matilda," Ben Cooper said, and grinned at her.

She glared at him.

"Mighty pretty," Ben repeated. His flannel shirt reeked of sweat and tobacco juice stained its collar. He had slicked back his hair, but his hands were permanently gray.

"Minding babies brings the glow," Mrs. Harris said. "Young'uns soften any girl's heart. You go tidy up, Matilda. Ben will wait for you by the fire, while I show these wee ones the new chicks."

Matty flew up the loft ladder, her heart banging against her chest. How long could she dawdle up here? She heard Ben thump over to the settle and the hiss of the fire when he spit on the hearth.

Slowly Matty brushed her hair and twisted it into a tight bun. It made her face look thin and pale. Good. Beneath her, Ben began to pace the floor. She eased herself down the ladder and walked toward the settle.

Matty sat down and spread out her skirts. Ben would have to take a bench. But he strode across the room, nudged her over, and took her hands.

"Miss Matilda, I'm so happy your ma gave us her blessing. She says you're too shy to speak for yourself.

But I like that. A woman should be quiet." Ben squeezed her hands. "Your ma says you don't want to wait until the new house is built, so just set the date."

"Don't—" she began, and pushed him away. Hard.

"Beg your pardon, Miss Matilda," Ben said.

"Matilda Anne!" Her mother rushed through the door and thrust the babies into her arms. "Shame!"

Matty stood. If she spoke her mind now, Ma would slap her in front of all of them, and she didn't need any more humiliating moments. One of the babies began to cry.

"Matilda," her mother called. "Where are your senses? Come make that baby a sugar tit." Mrs. Harris smiled at Ben. "I declare, your proposal has struck that girl speechless."

Matty slung the howling baby over her hip and stumbled to the hearth. The teakettle was steaming, and she poured a little water into a bowl with a bit of sugar. The baby still cried and snatched at her hair.

"Don't," Matty muttered. "Your pa's going to have to find some other ma for you."

CHAPTER
2

The next morning Ma handed Matty the egg basket. "Go see if you can find any more eggs for breakfast. You gathered early last night and those dominiques probably laid a couple in the far manger."

"But I checked there, Ma," Matty said.

"Well, check again. You're not known for careful searching," Ma said.

Matty stomped out of the cabin and flung open the barn door. She eyed the old rooster strutting through the oxen's stall and darted one hand beneath a sitting hen. Ben Cooper was like that rooster, puffed up and vain. She withdrew an egg and peeked into the far manger. Nothing.

Pausing on the path to the cabin, Matty picked up a goose feather, inspected it, and stuck it in her egg basket. She nudged open the cabin door and sniffed.

Sharp, rank smoke drifted from the fire. Her mother

squatted by the hearth, tossing something into the blaze. Matty squinted and dropped the egg basket.

"*No!*" she shrieked, and lunged toward her mother. Shoving her aside, she snatched at the flaming pieces of paper. Her copybook. Ashes of curled feathers littered the hearth and her fingers screamed as she pulled it out. She beat the paper against her skirt and sobbed.

"How could you? It's all I have," she wailed. Her fingers throbbed, but she curled them around the charred remnant, closing her eyes against the pain.

Mrs. Harris stood up and slapped Matty. "You foolish, willful girl. You could have sent both of us into the fire."

"But this is my book!" Matty cried, feeling it crumble in her hand.

"It's for your own good," Mrs. Harris said. "I'll have no more scribbling in this house. Or talk about more schooling. Ben Cooper will mend your headstrong ways."

"Never!" Matty snapped. "And you can't make me wed him." She spun around and ran toward the barn. Her fingers burned as she touched the rungs of the loft ladder, but she climbed up and onto the hay. Crawling, she reached the peak and slid down into a dark corner, thrust her fingers into her mouth, and wept.

Sometime later, she heard footsteps. "Matty." It was Abe. He began climbing the ladder. "Matty, Ma's gone. It was Mary Beth's time. It'll be awhile before that baby's born."

Hay slid down her neck. Matty uncurled, reached with her good hand, and Abe pulled her up.

"Let's see those fingers," Abe said, and cupped her hand in his. He shook his head. "Ma left goose grease out for you. Hurt much?"

Matty nodded. "When did she leave?"

"About an hour ago. Told me to split your table into kindling, but I brought it here."

"I'm leaving, Abe. Leaving now while Ma's away."

"Leaving?"

"Running away. To Mr. Spencer's school so I can scribble all I want." Matty reached into her pocket. "Ma may have burned my copybook, but she never found this. No one will take Mr. Nettleton's letter from me."

"What's so special about this school? Didn't Mr. Nettleton teach you enough?" Abe asked.

"No. A clerk needs to know so much more, commercial calculations, double-entry bookkeeping, and political economy. Mr. Nettleton had no time to teach me those."

"Couldn't you teach school? Mr. Nettleton could help you find a position. Ma might consent to teaching." Abe selected several pieces of straw and began to braid them together.

Matty rolled her eyes and snorted. "I'm going East, and I had best be starting before Ma brings a parson and Ben Cooper home."

"Not so hasty," Abe said, as he shaped the braid into a heart. "No proper woman goes marching down the turnpike. If your mind is set on this schooling, let me investigate a notion. I might be able to send you off in style."

"How?" Matty asked.

"I'll not be telling. Best wait."

"Oh, Abe." Matty sat up straight. "Tell me now, please? I'll die if I have to wait."

"Nope," Abe said. "You'll have to wait. Even penmen need patience."

"But why are you willing to help me? You usually don't go against Ma."

"I try to honor Ma," Abe answered, "but when I was your age I wanted to draw pictures. I begged Ma to find me a teacher, but she called that idea foolish, too. Said a man must work with his back. Seeing as I'm the head of the household now, I'll do what I can to help you."

Matty stared at her brother's worn hands. "Why did you stay?" she asked. "Didn't you feel like you were dying?"

"Ma needed me. And then I don't know, one day the longing was gone. Raising cows and training oxen can be satisfying."

"Ma doesn't deserve you," Matty said. She looked away and pressed her aching fingers to her cheek.

CHAPTER
3

"Matilda!" her mother shouted. "Make haste, girl! Abe's been waiting nigh ten minutes for you."

Matty's fingers shook as she stuffed the last pair of stockings into her basket and tied on her sunbonnet. A thread of fear wound itself around her insides. What if Abe's plan did not work? She backed down the loft ladder, trying to ease the basket after her, but it still banged against the ladder's rungs. She winced and waited.

"Hopeless girl. Will you never be careful?" Her mother snatched the basket and searched it. "You forgot the herbs I set out."

Matty clenched her teeth and picked up the herbs from the table. She paused and glanced around the cabin one last time. The logs were streaked with soot, and the holes in the chinking let in bits of sunlight that flickered on the dirt floor. Her eyes lingered on Teddy's blocks heaped by the hearth, and her heart twisted inside her. The cabin smelled of scorched lard and wet wool. She fled out-side—that part of home she would not miss.

"You best be mounting Abe's horse," her mother said. "I'll be out in a month and expect a good report. Be off with you now."

Matty hoped her mother would not discover her secret until the month was gone. She climbed up behind Abe, who urged his horse forward. Her younger broth-ers shouted good-bye. Matty blew Teddy a kiss and tried not to think of his soft touch.

The clearing and the cabin melted into the muted gray and green of the forest as they rode away. Only the scent of wood smoke seemed to follow them. At last Matty said, "I'm glad you hadn't given me your letter. I knew she'd search the basket. She never trusts me. Did she think I would take something that did not belong to me?"

"I don't think it was so much what you would take as what you would forget," Abe said. "And you *had* forgot-ten the herbs. Now don't lose this." He handed her a small envelope.

Matty tugged at Abe's sleeve. "Well? What's your plan? We're still headed for the Chapmans' farm, from what I can tell." She searched for the sun amid the canopy of the forest. "Do you think they'll tell Ma that I didn't come? I do regret leaving them without help. Ten children would wear a body out."

"Sorrowful enough to stay?" Abe asked and gave Matty a sidelong glance.

"Never." Matty shook her head. "They'll find someone else."

"Well, I'll go speak to them sometime soon." Abe slapped the reins. "We'll follow the creek until we meet the road to town."

Matty's heart began to beat faster. "Why town?"

"Remember Will Conner? He works in shipping on that new railroad. A while back I did him a good turn, and he offered to ship cargo East for me."

"Are you going to stow me away on a train?" Matty asked.

Abe chuckled. "You beat all, Matty, for your wild schemes. No, Will's giving us one of his family passes. It's a one-way ticket, so you'll be on your own when the schooling is completed."

Abe stopped to let his horse drink from the stream. The creek rippled over a snagged log. Matty rummaged in her basket and threw the packet of herbs into the current.

"Looks like you should have mended that sunbonnet," Abe said over his shoulder.

"Is it that bad?" Matty fiddled with the frayed ties and tried to push the threads back into place. "At least I won't need to wear a bonnet while I'm studying."

"That is true, but no proper woman would travel on a train without a bonnet," Abe remarked. "You may be running away, but you should still maintain a good character." His eyes narrowed as they met hers. "You remember that."

"This bonnet is all I have, so it will have to do," she said. They rode into a clearing brushed with a haze of purple lupines.

"Someday I'll be able to earn the money I need to buy decent clothing."

"Remember what Pa always quoted, *'Fortes fortuna adiuvat.'*" Abe glanced at Matty.

"*'Fortune helps the brave,'*" Matty murmured. "I don't feel brave, but I hope Fortune will still help me." Thinking about Pa jumbled everything inside her. Only he had shared her passion for words, but he had rarely been sober enough to temper Ma's scorn. "Pa did so love his Latin. It's such a pity that Ma sold his books. She wouldn't even allow me to keep one."

"She had to pay his debts somehow. We were fortunate to find a buyer. There's the Stewart farm. We'll be in town soon."

Matty gazed at the small homestead. Two spotted hogs rooted in a pen. A Jersey cow was staked out in a small pasture. Only three days ago she and Beth Stewart had graduated. Beth was to be married next month. Maybe if she had a young beau like Beth, marriage might be more appealing. But until that time she would rather be alone.

Abe interrupted her thoughts. "We have an extra hour or two. Will said to meet him at the station about four o'clock."

Abe guided his horse to a hitching post, tied the reins, and helped Matty off. "You look a little pale, Matty. Are you feeling poorly?"

"It's just my stomach. I couldn't eat much for breakfast." Matty took a deep breath. "I'm excited and scared."

Abe led her to a bench in front of the mercantile. "I would be scared, too, Matty, if I was running off." He looked into her eyes. "But I'll be praying for you. Think on that psalm that Mr. Nettleton read at graduation. 'He shall give his angels charge over thee, to keep thee in all thy ways.'"

Tears blurred her vision. How was she going to manage without Abe? Ever since Pa had died, he had been the one to give her hope.

Abe squeezed Matty's hand. "Come with me into the mercantile. I have a notion to buy you something."

"But you've already helped me so much."

Abe opened the door. "I think you need a proper bonnet."

Matty did not pause to check if any new calicos had arrived or to ask the prices of paper. Her feet pulled her straight to the millinery counter.

There were only three choices. Matty's hands instinctively raised a gray wool poke bonnet and tied it on. Abe chuckled.

"I calculated that you would choose that one." He held her by both shoulders and looked at her. "That gray makes your eyes seem greener."

"Oh, Abe, where did you find the money?" Matty bit her lip. He had so little saved for his own dreams, yet here he was, giving again to her.

"Out of my rail-splitting cash. Ma let me keep the last sum. Let's buy a bit of cheese and crackers for your trip." He tugged one of the bonnet's ribbons. "You can store that old sunbonnet for when you hoe Mrs. Spencer's garden."

Matty stood as straight as she could while Abe paid for the purchases. She had to learn to be a clerk. If she could be self-reliant, someday she would have enough money to buy Abe a gift.

"Might as well go to the depot," Abe said. He helped Matty onto his horse. "We can sit there and wait. More people come by here, and we don't want anyone to notice us." He mounted and guided the horse the few blocks to the train station.

"Ma is going to wonder where you are," Matty said.

"I told her I might stop by the Curtises' place and see if they needed any rails. They're clearing land for a new pasture."

"Are you sure there's not another reason?" Matty asked. A faint red crept up about his ears.

"Jenny Curtis is a fine young woman," Abe said. "But I'm not in a position to contemplate marriage."

"Me, either. Here comes Will Conner!" Will's boots stomped along the wooden platform.

"Here you are, Matty," Will said, pulling a green pasteboard ticket from his vest pocket. "A one-way pass to Ashtabula. Pay heed, you have to change trains in Toledo." He smiled and handed her the ticket.

The ticket burned in Matty's icy hand. She was truly bound for Ohio. All that she knew was remaining behind. The platform vibrated beneath her feet, and the pounding of her heart fell into the rhythm of the approaching train.

CHAPTER

4

✻

"Next car down is for ladies, miss," a porter explained. He waved Matty on, and the train began to move.

Matty stumbled along the aisle. Two rows of benches marched down the sides of the car. Her eyes traveled over families with squirming children and clusters of women in velvet who filled the seats. None of their calm faces seemed to match the tangled knot in her stomach. Maybe they all knew the place they were traveling toward. She inched her way forward until she found an unoccupied bench.

Everything dashed by quickly. There was barely time to focus on the trees and farms before they were lost from sight. They would be in Ohio in no time.

"Ticket, please, miss." Matty jerked around and looked up into the clean-shaven face of the conductor. "Your ticket, please," he repeated.

Hoping she looked as if she had ridden a train before, Matty dug into her basket and handed the man the pasteboard pass.

"You know you have to change trains in Toledo?" The conductor handed back her pass.

"Yes, sir. Do you know when we will arrive there?"

The conductor flipped open his watch. "Never can tell, miss. We're thirty minutes off schedule right now. And as windy as it is, we'll be losing more time." He shrugged and moved on.

Matty settled back into her seat. She retied the bow on her bonnet and smoothed her skirt. Despite the knots in her stomach, she was glad that the ticket was only good for travel one way. It would be harder for Ma to fetch her back, but she needn't worry about that yet. She sat up and looked about the railway car.

A young woman across the aisle held a baby while her husband read a newspaper. They looked as if they were going East to visit. Matty eyed the woman's short traveling jacket. Someday she might need one as a clerk. The baby reached toward his mother's face, just like Teddy did. Matty bit her lip.

She tried not to stare at the sober couple in front of her. The woman had on a gray wool dress with a wide, round, capelike collar that reached her waist. Her husband was plainly dressed in a black suit and wore a wide-brimmed black hat.

The train's whistle screeched, and Matty heard the hiss of breaks. The rocking slowed, and with a shudder the train stopped. "Overtown," called the conductor. A few passengers stood up and gathered their belongings before exiting the car.

Matty watched workmen load the fuel car for the train. It seemed to take hours. Finally the conductor called "all aboard," and the train's wheels began to turn.

She leaned back into her seat. If the train stopped this often, it would be morning before they reached Toledo.

Hours later the train chugged into Toledo. Matty packed away her shawl and hurried toward the aisle. Her toe hit a floorboard just as the train lurched. She tumbled forward, into the woman with the wide collar.

"I beg your pardon, ma'am. I didn't mean to push you. I tripped," Matty said.

"That you did. No harm done. Are you traveling alone?" The woman straightened Matty's bonnet.

"Yes, ma'am. I'm traveling to Ashtabula."

"How providential! We're switching to the same train." The woman patted Matty's hand. "I'm Martha Miller. You just stay with us and we'll see to your welfare."

"Pleased to meet you, ma'am. And thank you. I'm Matty Harris." The woman reminded Matty of a banty hen fussing over her chicks.

"Stay near," Mrs. Miller chirped. She picked up her skirt and descended the steps of the train.

Matty followed and stared at the crowds of people and carriages moving along the rows of shops. One store window was filled with shelves of books, while another shop displayed bolts of chintz, calicos, and percale. But there was no time to walk its aisles, rub her cheeks against the chintz, or smell the sizing. Instead she followed Mrs. Miller's black bonnet and boarded the train.

Mrs. Miller pulled out her knitting. "Will you be visiting relatives in Ashtabula?" she asked.

"No, ma'am. I plan to attend a seminary where clerks are trained," Matty answered.

Mrs. Miller stared at Matty. "Most unusual. How did you ever gain entry into such a school?"

"I haven't been accepted yet," Matty said. "But I do have a letter of recommendation."

"I see," Mrs. Miller murmured. She glanced over her knitting at Matty. "And if you are not accepted?"

Matty's heart froze. She tried to swallow while the wheels beneath her raced over the few remaining miles.

"I don't know, ma'am," she said, and her voice faltered.

CHAPTER

5

✳

Matty slowed her steps and eyed the white clapboard house cloaked in honeysuckle vines. Maples shaded the homestead, and a formal garden graced the yard. Next to the house stood a large barn with a duck pond off to one side. The farm matched Mr. Nettleton's description. Her fingers shook as she straightened her bonnet.

She had traveled so far and had looked forward to this moment for days. But what would she do if Mr. Spencer would not accept her as a student? She couldn't go home. She had to convince him.

A dump cart with a team of oxen was parked in the farm lane. Matty tried to squeeze past the cart but caught her petticoat on the split-rail fence. As she stooped to unsnag the ruffle, she heard screams.

"Henry! Harvey! I'll get back at you for this!" shrieked a boy. He stumbled out of the duck pond and shook himself.

"Thought you needed a little cooling off, Lyman," teased an older boy. He tossed back his curls and laughed. From behind the oxcart someone else laughed.

"You said you wished Pa'd let us go swimming," the other boy said. He backed up and stumbled over Matty. "Oh, I'm sorry, miss," he said.

"You're twins!" Matty gasped. She nodded toward the other boy. They were both a foot taller than her and at least a year older.

"We're Henry and Harvey," one boy said with a grin.

"Who's who?" Matty asked.

"That is the question, isn't it?" The boy laughed. "And who are you? Are you lost?"

"Maybe. I don't know. I'm looking for the home of Platt Rogers Spencer." Matty licked her lips. These boys seemed as rascally as her brothers, maybe even worse.

"This is it. He's my pa. Phebe, run and tell Ma there's a girl here." A younger girl tumbled off the load of hay and ran toward the house.

At the twin's words Matty squared her shoulders and walked toward the house. She wished he had called her a young lady. If Mr. Spencer thought she was only a child, he would send her home. A door slammed, and a tall woman approached her.

"May I help you?" a gentle voice called. Matty looked up at the dark-haired woman with a toddler clinging to her skirt. Peaceful brown eyes scanned Matty, and the woman smiled. "Yes?"

Matty's mouth was dry, and she struggled to swallow. "Are you Mrs. Spencer?" Matty asked. "I'm Matty Harris. I've come to ask if I may study at Mr. Spencer's Log Cabin Seminary. I have letters of recommendation from my brother and from Mr. Nettleton, Mr. Spencer's own former teacher."

Matty stood twisting a bonnet string while Mrs. Spencer read the letters. She hoped Abe's letter sounded convincing. And what would she say if Mrs. Spencer questioned her about her mother? It would be a long, hungry walk back to Michigan and Ma's schemes.

Mrs. Spencer glanced at her other daughter. "Phebe, would you please look after Ellen?"

Phebe made a face at the toddler. "Can't catch me!" She dashed off toward the barn with Ellen chasing her.

"Are you old enough to be here, Matilda? Usually the seminary students are eighth-grade graduates who come to study business skills. And most are boys."

"Oh, I have graduated, ma'am. I'm just small for my age. I'll be fifteen in November. But I haven't any money. I heard sometimes Mr. Spencer lets his students work off their tuition. I was hoping he would let me do that, please, ma'am," Matty added.

"Fifteen in November, a mite young, but there are others your age. We already have two older boys working for their tuition, so we shall wait and see what Mr. Spencer says. For tonight you may stay with us. Pray follow me inside." Mrs. Spencer motioned toward the house, and Matty followed her down a brick path edged with phlox. All about the house bloomed larkspur and pansies.

"Where did you come from, Matilda?" Mrs. Spencer asked.

Matilda! How she hated that name, the one her mother always called her. Even though it might sound more adult, she'd be glad to be shut of it. "I'm from near Manlius, Michigan. And, ma'am, might you please call me Matty?" Matty was Abe's pet name for her. She paused to smell one of the maroon roses arching over the kitchen door as she and Mrs. Spencer entered.

"Certainly, Matty. Mr. Spencer wanted this rose," Mrs. Spencer said, fingering the blossoms. "It reminds him of his favorite Robert Burns song, 'O My Luve's Like a Red, Red Rose.' But come in and have something to drink."

Mrs. Spencer held the kitchen door open. "Set your bundle in the far room at the top of the stairs. That's where Sara sleeps."

Matty stood in the dining room at the bottom of the stairs. A blue-and-white tea set sat on a cherry sideboard. She could even see her reflection in the polished top of the table, from which a large bouquet of roses scented the air. Matty ran her hand along the rungs of a high-backed chair. She was truly here, in the home of the greatest penman in America.

At the top of the stairs Matty turned toward the last room. It had to be the correct one. Those wild boys wouldn't sleep under a pink-and-green quilt. A calico cat rested on the bed. When Matty entered the room, the cat lifted her head, stretched one paw, and went back to sleep.

The room smelled of lavender. Matty stared at the rose leaf stenciling that bordered the walls. What a heavenly room, so cheery and bright, how unlike her pallet in the corner of the loft back home. She had always slept with onions and beans drying from the rafters, so close they almost touched her nose.

Matty took off her shoes and examined a blister on one heel. Someday she'd wear shoes that were made especially for her. She slid her feet along the smooth planed boards. At least here there'd be no more splinters in her toes. She hung her basket on a peg and noticed some writing on the wall. Grasses and ferns were interlocked with a pair of initials.

"Sara Spencer," Matty murmured.

She turned to the gabled window and looked out. Apple trees reached up toward her. Their gray-green leaves rippled in a breeze. A brook bordered the orchard, and geese splashed in the rills. How different from the scraggly clearing around their gloomy cabin.

A little spring seemed to well up inside her, and Matty felt her shoulders relax. Even if she had to beg Mr. Spencer to keep her, she would. Here was the home of her dreams.

"Matty," she heard Mrs. Spencer call, and feeling taller than her usual five feet, she ran down the stairs.

"Would you like cool mint tea or water, Matty?" Mrs. Spencer asked. "The tea's been in the springhouse."

"The tea would be nice, please, ma'am." Matty glanced around the kitchen. Bunches of pennyroyal and savory hung from the rafters and made the room smell sweet and earthy. In one corner hung a birdcage. The bird inside it began to trill.

"How pretty! Is it a canary? I've never seen one before." Matty peeked into the cage.

"He belongs to Sara, our eldest daughter. She named him Robin Goodfellow, after Shakespeare's character." Mrs. Spencer handed Matty a glass of tea. "That's Sara walking up the lane. She's been at the seminary correcting papers for her father."

Sara eyed Matty when she entered the kitchen. "Who do we have here?" she asked. Matty's shoulders tightened. If Sara and she were to room together, she'd best make a favorable impression.

"Matty Harris," Mrs. Spencer answered. "She would like to enroll in Papa's school. I asked her to spend the night, since your father and I will have to discuss the matter." She wiped her forehead with her apron. "Sara,

I'm a bit behind with supper. Could you and Matty pod these peas for me, please?"

"Certainly," Sara said. She picked up a basket and handed Matty two bowls. "Let's go to the grape arbor." Matty trailed after Sara.

"Here we are," Sara said. She settled herself on the white arbor bench. All about them hung little clusters of green grapes, their vines clinging to white lattice.

Matty tucked her feet under her skirt and glanced at Sara. Sara's black hair was brushed back and neatly covered her ears like two crow's wings. From her oval face two blue eyes met Matty's green eyes.

"Have you ever been away from home?" Sara asked.

"No, Miss Sara," Matty said. She smoothed her hair a bit lower over her ears. Someday she'd sew a fitted gown similar to Sara's and wear a silver brooch. Sara must think her a woodsy, dressed in brown calico.

"Please don't call me 'Miss,'" interrupted Sara. "I'm not that much older than you, and since we may spend the summer together, we might as well consider ourselves friends. So this is your first time away from home?"

"Yes, I'm the only girl, so Ma always needed my help," Matty answered. She watched Sara's soft hands as they reached for more pea pods. Her own hands were calloused, but at least her fingers were healing. She'd have to ask Sara for some lard to rub into her skin. Matty split a pod with her nail and rolled the peas into her bowl.

"What about your father?" Sara asked.

"He was killed in a logging accident two winters ago. But we've managed." Matty threw a handful of pods into the basket. If managing meant having Ma grow more sour every day.

"I'm sorry about your father," Sara said. "It'll certainly be nice if you can stay. Papa's scholars this summer are all boys. I hope they take kindly to a girl invading their classroom." Sara gave Matty a sidelong glance. "And beware of the twins. No one escapes their tricks."

"I met them first. They'd just thrown some other boy into the duck pond," Matty said.

Sara chuckled. "That was probably Lyman. He's the artist of the family. Those twins should have been named 'frolic and foolery.' They're always up to mischief. Have you come to prepare for teaching a school?" Sara asked.

"Absolutely not. Teachers are always poor. I want to be a penman and work for a business," Matty answered.

Sara raised her eyebrows. "Well, Papa believes that women should have a fair chance to learn business skills, but most businesses only hire men for clerks."

"That may be, but somewhere, someone is going to hire me," Matty said.

"You haven't met Papa yet?" Sara asked.

"No, just your mother. What's it like to have a famous father who's sold thousands of books?" Matty asked. "Does everyone stare at you and point when you go to town?"

"No." Sara laughed. "Our neighbors know that Papa's called the Father of American Penmanship. They read his poetry in the newspapers, but in Ashtabula County we're merely the Spencers. And Papa's fame has not always been a blessing. He used to be away for weeks teaching penmanship."

"Then who ran the farm?" Matty thought of her own family's labors to farm without a father. Each year it seemed her mother's shoulders drooped more and her temper quickened.

"Mama and us children. My older brother, Robert, was home then."

The rumble of wheels sounded from behind the barn. "I think I hear Papa and the boys coming," Sara said. "Those oxen always want to run when they know it's their last load. It sure rattles the cart. Here, you take these to Mama, and I'll dump the pods."

Matty carried the bowl of peas into the kitchen. She sniffed the air. Fried chicken, and it was only Tuesday! She noticed a shaggy-haired man wearing spectacles, standing near a window. The back of his farm smock was covered with bits of hay.

The man certainly was grubby for being a Master Penman. He must be reading one of the letters she had brought.

"You are Miss Harris, I assume? I am Platt Rogers Spencer," he said, and offered her his hand.

"I am honored to meet you, sir," Matty answered, and shook his hand. Her whole body felt frozen, and her tongue could barely move. The pounding of her heart almost drowned out his words.

"Well then, Miss Harris, Mr. Nettleton wrote you a fine recommendation," Mr. Spencer said. "He says that your determination and common sense compensate for your beginner's skill."

Matty stammered, "Mr. Nettleton has always been kind to me, sir. It was his idea that I come here and study with you."

"Years ago Mr. Nettleton was the first person who believed in me," Mr. Spencer said. "He allowed me to write out all his copy slips, and here I am, forty years later, still handing out copy slips for students to learn from. Why do you want to study at my school?"

"I want to earn money," Matty blurted out. "I mean, sir, I want to help my family. Ever since my father died, we've struggled to pay for our farm. I thought maybe I would earn more as a clerk than if I went into teaching."

"Good practical answers," Mr. Spencer said. "But I was hoping that I might hear that the smell of the ink and a love of letters lured you to my door. There is only room in my seminary for the dedicated. Those who are passionate about learning."

Matty paled. He thought her a superficial girl, unworthy of his time. "I do love writing your letters, and I want to be a clerk, but I need more training. Please, sir, may I stay?"

Mr. Spencer sighed. "The seminary is crowded this summer, and you would be the only girl. I don't know how we can make any more room."

Her heart seemed to rise into her throat and cut off her breathing. She couldn't go home. And she was used to being the only girl in a horde of boys. "Please, sir, please let me stay. I can prove that I am worthy of a place. Please?"

"I suppose I could allow you to remain on a trial basis." Mr. Spencer ran his fingers through his hair. "In a month or so we shall assess your progress," he said.

"Thank you, sir!" Matty gasped. "Thank you." Certainly she could prove herself. And by the end of the summer she'd be ready for a clerking position.

"Come now," Mr. Spencer said. "Here is your first lesson." He took something from his pocket and placed it in her hand.

Matty squinted and moved her hand into a shaft of sunlight. A granite pebble lay in her palm. Flecks of mica caught the sunlight and glittered.

"That's the shape you must always keep in mind, the oval of a pebble found on Lake Erie's shore. There are no more perfect shapes than the ones nature has given us. Those are the shapes that must flow through your letters. And tomorrow you will make them with your pen."

CHAPTER
6

Matty slumped in her seat at a makeshift desk and glanced about the Jericho Log Cabin Seminary. The windows along the north wall allowed a stream of sunshine into the center of the log cabin. The wooden floor was scratched from the movement of chairs and heavy boots. All the other scholars were boys, a mixture of farm and town lads, clothed in checks and chambray. They sat at long tables covered with ink pots, quills, and paper, their long legs in a tangle and blocking the aisles. They all cast perturbed looks at her and especially at her feet, dangling inches above the floor.

Matty clenched her teeth together. She must ignore them, just pretend they weren't there. But what was she going to do about her feet? In her mind Matty could envision the sketch from her copybook of an earnest penmanship student, body erect, soles firmly on the floor, but her feet just would not reach. One of the boys snickered, and her cheeks grew warm.

A cool hand touched her shoulder. "Is something wrong, Matty?" Sara asked.

"My feet don't touch the floor, Sara," Matty whispered.

"Hmm, don't worry, Matty. Papa will have an idea." Sara bustled to the front of the room.

Matty watched while Sara whispered to Mr. Spencer, who then motioned to Lyman. Lyman listened attentively to his father and hastened out of the school.

"Class," Mr. Spencer said. "Before we take up our pens I'd like to remind you of the importance of rhythm. Just as a steady beat is crucial in music, we as penmen must maintain an even rhythm. So this morning we shall begin with a song." Mr. Spencer nodded at Matty and then taking up a pointer strode to the blackboard. "We shall use the tune of 'Auld Lang Syne.' Let's begin." He hummed a note and the class hesitantly joined in singing:

Hail, servant Pen, to thee we give,
Another pleasant hour—
'Tis thine to bid our memories live,
And wave our thoughts in flowers!

The pen, the pen, the brave old pen,
Which stamped our thoughts of yore,
Through its bold tracings oft again,
Our thought will freshly pour.

Then be thy movements bold and true,
Friend of the laboring mind;

Light, shade, form entrance the view,
And glow thro' every line.

A few guffaws erupted at the end of the song. While the other students commented on Mr. Spencer's latest variation, Lyman arrived at Matty's seat.

"Place these under your feet," he said, holding out two large flat stones.

"Thank you, Lyman," Matty answered, and positioned the stones so her feet could rest on them. More snickers and snorts sounded around her. Matty sat up straight and focused on her inkwell. If only Mr. Spencer would hand out copy slips so they could begin working.

"Silence, class," Mr. Spencer said. "Let's see how agile your minds are. Can you decipher today's Latin phrase?"

Matty stared at the blackboard. She had been so involved in her woes that she had missed the phrase.

Mr. Spencer read aloud, *"Vox audita perit, littera scripta manet."* He sounded like her father.

The Latin words drew her mind back to winter evenings by the hearth. Hiding in the shadows, she had listened to her father's voice quote Virgil. *"Arma virumque cano, Troiae qui primus ab orbis."* His deep voice had made the words vibrate within her and cast images of ancient Rome upon her imagination.

But the rum in his pewter mug had thickened her father's words and drained him of his intellect and integrity.

"Come now," Mr. Spencer's voice pulled Matty back to the present. "Can no one figure out the remaining words? What does it mean?"

Matty raised her hand. "'The spoken word dies, the written letter remains.' It means, sir, what we write will remain longer than the words we speak, which flee away."

"*Bene*, Miss Harris," Mr. Spencer said. "Mr. Nettleton taught you well."

"Mr. Nettleton was a good teacher, sir. But my father spoke Latin at home and often quoted from Virgil's *Aeneid*."

"Can you believe that?" The boy beside her muttered to the fellow next to him. "Who ever heard of a girl being a penman? I bet within the week she'll be crying her way home."

Matty eyed the blond boy who had spoken. His companion shook his head. "But it would be an asset to have a clever head like that." The boy gazed at her for a moment and nodded.

Matty played with her quill and wished they'd change the subject.

"Scholars," Mr. Spencer said. "This is not a time for conversation. Eyes forward. We shall begin with a review. Remember that all the letters in my script are based on four principles. We have the straight line running at a forty-five-degree angle, an under-curve, the overcurve, and lastly the extended loop.

"For example, the union of principles three, two, and one gives us the lower case *a*." Mr. Spencer's arm swept up in the overcurve and then continued with an under-curve to complete the *a*. A final fluid stroke drew the angled straight line that began another *a*. "Now you try," said Mr. Spencer. He ran his chalk-dusted hands through his graying black hair. He and Sara began to walk slowly around the room.

Matty's hand shook as she picked up her quill. She breathed deeply and tried to remember how her arm should feel when moving correctly. She dipped her quill in her ink and attempted a few *a*'s. Lint clogged the quill's point, but she did not wipe it. Instead she dashed off several more lines of letters. She'd show those boys she was as good as they were. The scent of rosewater drifted about her, and Matty realized that Sara was watching. "They're not correct," Matty muttered.

"Patience, Matty," Sara said. She cleaned the quill's point. "This is only your first day. Why don't you attempt this exercise? It might help you find your rhythm."

Sara sat down next to Matty and wrote a chain of letters.

"Think of treadling a spinning wheel. Just as you try to treadle smoothly, your arm needs to move in a circular

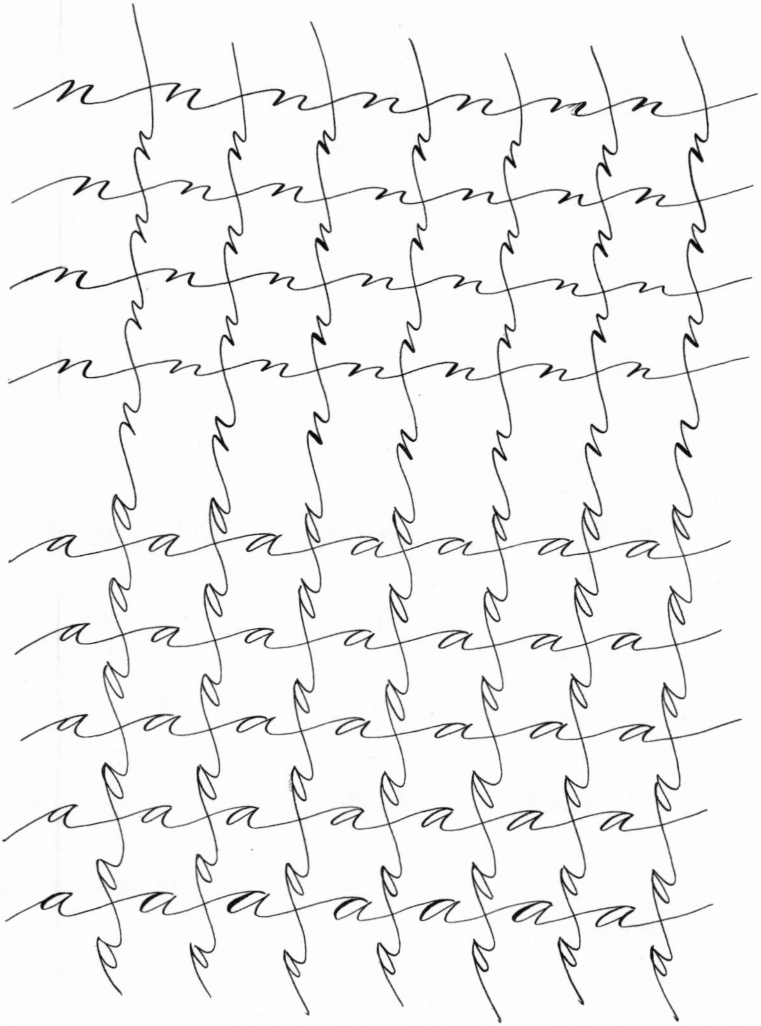

motion across your paper." Sara's arm swept across the paper with the same fluid motion her father had used.

"Do you have a steel pen, Matty? You could try it instead of your quill."

"No, I had one my father used, but the pen point was worn."

"That's a common problem," Sara said. "Plus Papa says you can never achieve a smoothly shaded letter with a straight penholder. He always uses a quill. But one of the twins is trying to design a penholder as good as a quill." Sara stood up and offered her chair to Mr. Spencer before going to answer another student's question.

"That particular twin has some remarkable ideas," Mr. Spencer said. "We think it is Harvey, although the twins never tell us who is who. Feet squarely on the floor?"

"Thank you, sir," Matty said. She might look ridiculous, but the stones did solve one of her problems.

Outside the log cabin a bobwhite called. Mr. Spencer sniffed the air. "You can smell the hay curing even in here. Where's your pebble, Matty?"

She took it from her apron pocket and placed it on her desk. Mr. Spencer pulled up a chair next to her. "Memorize this shape. Close your eyes and draw it in your mind. Then let it flow out your fingers and through your pen."

Mr. Spencer checked her quill. "I'll trim it in a minute, but let me show you one of Harvey's pens." He held out an odd-looking pen. "He gave this to me a few nights ago."

Instead of the pen point being held by the end of the wooden shaft, there was a small copper arm set to one side at the end of the pen. A pen point could be inserted into the arm.

"Rather peculiar-looking, isn't it? But the oblique angle of that arm allows this pen to write with the flexibility of a quill. I'll show you."

By now all twelve students had risen to watch Mr. Spencer. They crowded around Matty's desk. One of the boys pointed at the stones and elbowed his friend.

"Does that pen have a name, sir?" a boy asked.

"Harvey calls it his oblique pen." Rapidly Mr. Spencer moved his whole right arm. Matty caught her breath. For in a web of lacelike letters Platt Rogers Spencer had flourished her name.

"How pretty," said a voice from behind her. Matty recognized the voice as the one who had praised her earlier.

Someone giggled and pointed at the blackboard. "Lyman's been at it again. Will you look at that!" All the boys began to laugh.

Matty gasped. It was a cartoon of her! A miniature Matty sat swinging her legs many inches above the floor. Her desk towered over her, and the cartoon character struggled to lift a giant-size quill.

"Lyman, erase that nonsense this instant," commanded his father. Mr. Spencer strode to the front of the room.

"He sure can draw," said the blond boy. "Anybody can tell it's that pint-size girl."

"Scholars, back to your seats. It's high time you practiced your penmanship," Mr. Spencer said. "There has been too much foolishness today."

Matty pressed her lips together and stared at her paper. The shapes of the letters blurred. It was her fault. Mr. Spencer would not let her stay if he thought she distracted the boys.

"Please don't hold this against Lyman, Matty," Sara whispered. "He's a scalawag, like the twins."

Matty nodded and dipped her pen.

CHAPTER

7

✳

Only two weeks had passed, but Matty wished she could live with the Spencers forever. Housekeeping with Sara was actually fun. If only there was a way to appease those boys. Their schoolroom pranks struck deeper than any of her brothers' tricks, and neither praise nor advice seemed to alter their antagonism.

She hastened into the pantry and filled a bowl with apple butter for the breakfast table. Out of the small paned window she saw Phebe running toward the house.

"Ma!" cried Phebe as she dashed into the kitchen. Tears streaked her face. "One of the twins opened the door while I was in the outhouse and threw green apples at me!" Phebe blew her nose on her pinafore, which was spotted with stains.

Matty stepped back while Mrs. Spencer rushed to the kitchen door. "Henry! Harvey! Come here this minute." From around the corner of the house walked the two boys with their hands in their pockets. "Well," Mrs. Spencer said. "Which one of you was it this time?"

Sara chuckled. "You know they won't tell." She rolled her eyes and shook her head.

"She started it," one of the twins said. He made a face at Phebe. "She kept poking a stick through a knothole when I was in the outhouse yesterday."

"It is not your place to punish Phebe," Mrs. Spencer said, and placed a hand on the boy. "You two torment Phebe and Lyman constantly. You need to practice charity with one another. Besides, you should never open the outhouse door while anyone is inside."

Mrs. Spencer turned to her daughter. "And to think that one of my daughters should act in such a low and unladylike manner. Shame on you, Phebe, for engaging in such rudeness! You shall be punished."

Phebe's face contorted, and she began to cry. She pushed aside the screen door and ran to the barn.

Mrs. Spencer opened her mouth and then pressed her lips together. "Sometimes I don't know what to do with that child," she said, and went back to ladling sausage gravy into a bowl. Through the open doorway Matty watched Mr. Spencer carry in two pails of milk. Phebe marched beside him.

"Persis, my love and my dove," Matty heard Mr. Spencer say quietly. "I think we are all in need of a holiday. A little bird told me that her mama was not her gentle self."

Mrs. Spencer brushed a hand over her forehead. "I reckon I was a bit harsh with Phebe. It must be this heat. What are you plotting this morning, Platt?"

"Why not take the school to the lake? Your favorite wild strawberry patch is near the shore. We'll all lend a hand with the picking once our lessons are done."

Matty's hands flew to her mouth. Even though she needed all the learning she could glean, a day free from classroom pranks would be heavenly. She'd have the dishes washed and the crumbs swept before the first student from town arrived.

From the kitchen she heard Phebe speak. "I'm sorry, Mama. I'll try harder not to tease the boys."

"And please forgive me, my child," Mrs. Spencer said. "I'm sorry that I lost my temper and spoke in such a rash manner." Mrs. Spencer hugged Phebe and kissed her cheek.

Matty stared at the mother and daughter. Mrs. Spencer's gentle words echoed in her head. Never had her own mother spoken thus to her. Like a kettle of milk, her mother's anger would boil over. If she had misbehaved, her mother would still be raging.

Matty grabbed for the forks, missed, and the cutlery clattered to the floor. Mrs. Spencer jerked about and gazed at the scrambled silverware. Her shoulders quivered, and she began to laugh. "Only half past six, and such a morning! Mind the china, Matty, it's not as tolerant as the silver."

* * *

A few hours later Matty steadied herself as her feet slipped on the pine-needle-covered path. The game trail twisted through the underbrush of elderberries and bracken. Sunbeams flickered through the gaps left by the hemlocks and beech trees that shaded the slopes. The flutelike call of the wood thrush rippled through the air, and Matty stopped to listen. These woods did not seem as gloomy as the ones at home.

"Why don't you let me carry that basket?" a low voice said. Matty turned and recognized Phineas Stewart, the boy who had nodded to her.

"Thank you," she said.

"Have you seen Lake Erie before?" he asked.

"No, have you?" Matty's cheeks flushed.

"Once, a few weeks ago, just after I came. I hiked over on a Sunday afternoon. The woods near the lake were white with Dutchmen's britches. The May apples were blooming, too. They reminded me of my family's farm back home."

"Where did you come from?" Matty asked.

"Near Pittsburgh. What about you? Did you attend a ladies seminary back East?"

"I'm from Michigan."

"What is your father doing there? Most men who can quote Virgil don't end up in the backwoods of Michigan."

"My father was originally from New York. He came west to teach Latin at Oberlin College, but after my parents married, they moved north."

46

Phineas laughed. "How odd that a Latin master should decide to farm. What does your father think of you coming here?"

"My father died two winters ago," said Matty. She bit her lip and glanced away. Pa would have understood why she had to come here.

"I'm sorry," said Phineas. "My pa was against my coming. He says men do not sit at desks all day. They sweat when they work."

"Then how did you convince him to allow you to come?" Matty asked. Phineas held back a low branch and let her pass first.

"I broke my leg back in the winter. My brother dared me to walk across the roof rafters we were nailing, and I fell. I kept on pestering Pa about coming here until he relented. He said, since I wouldn't be worth much on the farm this summer, I might as well study clerking."

Matty looked up into his tanned face. Phineas's gray-blue eyes were the color of the pewter cup her father had brought from New York. There was none of Abe's solemnity in those eyes, but rather a recklessness that sparkled. If only she could be equally as bold. "Does your leg still hurt you?" she asked.

"A mite, but sometimes it's handy to pursue a slower gait," he said.

Matty blushed. No boy had ever said such a thing to her.

"Matty," called Sara from far ahead. "Make haste. I want to watch your face when you first see the lake."

"Go on," Phineas said, and smiled. "I need to rest. I'll catch up in a bit." He eased himself down and leaned against a tree.

"Thank you for carrying the basket," Matty said, and turned back to the trail. She could hear gulls, and her heart soared with their cries. She tried to hurry, but the hem of her skirt was caught. She tugged at it and heard it tear.

"Bother," Matty mumbled. When she tried to turn around, she fell over. The boy whose foot had been on her skirt snorted.

"Why don't you take your skirts and petticoats back to where you belong! We don't need any girls in our class," Caleb said. He pushed her aside, and a branch slapped Matty in the face. Matty glared at him.

The woods thinned at the edge of a small cliff, and when Matty reached the crest where Sara waited, a gust of wind swept their faces and blew back their sunbonnets. Endless lines of waves rose and fell, their whitecaps sliding into silver troughs and rising again. A flotilla of ducks rode the waves while sandpipers raced along the shore.

Matty gasped. "I would never have imagined such a great quantity of water! I can't even see the other side."

"No, you goose. This is a great big lake. They used to call them the English Seas."

"An inland sea," Matty murmured. "I wonder what it's like to sail on such a lake?"

"Ask Papa. Before he married Mama he was a clerk on a ship. He sailed all over Lake Erie. And can you imagine, he drew letters on the walls and deck of the ship!"

Matty giggled. "I can't imagine your father kneeling on the deck, flourishing someone's initials. Was the captain angry?"

"I don't believe so. Now that he's famous, the crew probably points out those letters to the passengers. 'The only ship flourished by the Master Penman, Platt Rogers Spencer,'" quoted Sara in a low voice. "Come, everyone's already at the shore." Together they slid down the incline, which was littered with fragments of shale.

At the bottom Mattie closed her eyes and listened. The gravel hissed as the surf sucked pebbles into the undertow. An eddy of wind hurled sand against her cheeks and grit onto her lips. She strolled the beach and watched the boys wrestling near the water. The spray from their splashing caught the sunlight, and a rainbow drifted over the waves.

Mr. and Mrs. Spencer walked up ahead, arm in arm. Platt Rogers Spencer smiled tenderly at Persis, and Matty watched as he wrote in the sand:

Persis Spencer 1853

Mrs. Spencer laughed and called out, "Dinner!"

The students rushed toward the food like a school of bluegill after a worm. Matty helped Persis and Sara pass out the picnic, and when Phineas took his plate, her hand shook.

After the picnic, Mr. Spencer brushed the crumbs from his beard and stood up. "Even though it is a perfect day for reciting poetry . . ." He paused until the moans had subsided. "I've decided to waive the poetry, but not the penmanship lesson."

He laid two pebbles on the sand and traced around them with a stick. "Here is the basic shape for the capital letters *S* and *G*." Mr. Spencer removed the stones and drew the letters mentioned. "The first place I practiced my letters was here, where I originally envisioned them. And now I want you to trace letters in Erie's sand. Remember to use your whole arm as you write. Your arm should move like one of those waves."

Matty and the other students picked up sticks and dropped to their knees. Matty stared at the pebbles in front of her. She stiffened her wrist and drew a series of ovals.

"Not bad, Miss Harris," Mr. Spencer said. He squatted down next to her, while Sara walked about and checked the other students' work.

"Truly? My shapes seem too lopsided. I can't match your letters. I never had enough paper at home to practice on."

"Neither did I," Mr. Spencer said. "And I even spent the first cent I ever earned on a sheet of paper, I longed for it so. I was only eight at the time. A neighbor was going to town, and he offered to buy the paper for me. We lived a long way from town, and it was late at night when the man returned. But I was still awake listening for the lift of the latchstring. I snatched the roll of paper from him and smoothed it out by our hearth. I picked up my brother's quill, dipped it, and began to write. Somehow the letters in my head just didn't resemble the shapes I drew. I was so disappointed that I pitched the mess in a corner and went to bed."

"What was wrong?" Matty fiddled with the twig she was using. A few of the boys had stopped practicing and were also listening.

"I needed more patience with myself. I knew what I wanted to write, but my muscles and mind needed more practice before I could truly draw the letters I envisioned. Do not be so hasty. I think I need to give you some extra homework." Mr. Spencer rubbed his chin. "It seems you still have not mastered what we learned in the first week. Keep practicing. I expect you shall have learned them before I decide if you may stay for the remainder of the summer."

CHAPTER
8

"Ouch!" Matty cried, and dropped the hot quill on the kitchen table. She stuck her fingers in her mouth and glared at the crock of heated sand used for curing the feathers. Those dratted boys were at fault. If only they'd leave her supply of quills alone, but once again she had found her quills bent and broken. It was a miracle that Sara hadn't asked why she needed so many feathers. Someone nudged the kitchen door open, and Matty looked up.

Phineas dropped his armload of wood into the woodbox and scanned the scene. "Why don't you let me teach them a lesson, Matty? I could pour paste in their inkwells or fill their quills with manure."

Matty frowned. "Sometimes I think of such tricks, but I'll not stoop to their ways." If she could not conquer these boys, how could she succeed in the business world? After all, she had never given in to her brothers' teasing.

"Well, at least allow me the pleasure of trimming your quill." Phineas picked up the feather and with his thumbnail, scraped the fine skin off the feather's shaft. He pulled a wooden-handled knife from a case in his pocket and began to shape a point. "Does Mr. Spencer still not know how the other boys pester you?" he asked.

"No! And don't tell him! He already feels I'm a distraction." Matty sighed. "I think Sara knows. But she has not said anything to me." Matty plopped down on a chair and watched Phineas. The tip of his tongue edged out of a corner of his mouth as he concentrated on his knife. At last he splayed the end of the quill on his thumbnail and nodded.

"You did a good job curing this quill," Phineas said, and handed Matty the feather, but he did not release his grasp on it. "Better hide this one, or accept my methods of dealing with the transgressors."

"No," Matty said, and he let go of the feather. "I have to lick them on my own."

The next morning before school began Matty set a vase with a red rose on Mr. Spencer's desk and slipped into her desk with her new quill safe in her apron pocket. She eyed her inkwell. At least the boys had left that alone last night. She would not have to endure their snickers when asking Mr. Spencer for more ink. He must think she drank it!

And her stones were in place. Maybe the boys were growing weary of hiding them. Matty sat down. When she placed her feet on the stones, something scuttled beneath her skirts.

"*EEEEK!*" she screamed, and jumped from her desk. All around her laughter rumbled. She shook her skirt, and a salamander darted across the floor. She raised her foot and then set it back down.

Mr. Spencer entered and glanced about the room. "I apologize for my tardiness, scholars, but trust that you set to work. One of our cows was calving, and my presence was needed. We shall forego our opening exercises and begin with this drill."

Matty examined her copy slip and began to write a row of *L*'s. Over and over she dipped her quill and copied the letters with their accompanying motto. Despite the early morning hour, sweat trickled between her shoulder blades and her arm was beginning to ache.

Matty raised her hand and Mr. Spencer nodded at her. "May I be excused for a drink, sir?"

"Certainly," Mr. Spencer said, and went back to assisting Jehu.

Matty walked to the back of the room, poured a dipper of water, and looked about. Phineas was working hard, but a few fellows barely moved their quills. Caleb yawned, rubbed his wrist, and blew across his paper to dry the ink. Everyone's shirt-sleeves were rolled up, and Mr. Spencer kept mopping his brow.

"Class," Mr. Spencer said, and untied his cravat. "I perceive that the heat has addled your ability to concentrate this morning. I suggest we lay aside these drills and commence with something different." He strode to the front of the room and set his cravat on his desk.

"You know that penmen often challenge each other as to who can create the most lavish flourish. I propose such a contest. You will have thirty minutes to design a flourish and execute it. The creator of the best flourish will be awarded one of the twin's new oblique pens."

Matty chewed her lower lip and played with a strand of her hair. Mr. Spencer had taught them how to flourish a cartouche and different birds last week. Probably everyone would draw one of those designs. She dipped her quill and drew two graceful parallel lines. With swift strokes Matty added a bouquet of grasses and wheat above the lines. Now for a motto, but which one?

Matty flipped through a stack of copy slips and found one she had enjoyed. Without cleaning the dried ink from her quill, she lettered out the verse. While waiting for the ink to dry, Matty leaned back in her chair and looked out the window. Swallows swooped for insects; their flight seemed to mimic the darting motions of the other scholars' pens.

Mr. Spencer cleared his throat. "Sign your papers, and please bring them to my desk."

Gems of price are deeply hidden
Neath the rugged rocks concealed
What would ne'er come forth unbidden
To Thy search may be revealed.

Matty signed her name, but just as she lifted her quill, someone bumped her elbow. Her hand smeared part of her work, and the quill scratched across a corner of her paper. Matty gasped and looked up.

"Beg your pardon, miss," Jehu stammered. "Pity about your paper." He lumbered down the aisle.

Matty sat rigid and stared at his back. Jehu was clumsy, but had someone asked him to bump her? She looked about the room. Caleb and Thomas were smirking at each other. She hated them. Hated them! She shoved back her chair and marched to Mr. Spencer's desk. He'd just think her hasty again.

CHAPTER

9

❀

Later that evening Matty jerked open the corner cupboard door. She knelt down and riffled through the maze of bottles and small boxes. The red pepper had to be near the front, because Mrs. Spencer had used it yesterday. She shoved aside several tins and spied the pepperbox. Matty snatched it and stuffed it in her apron pocket. Jumping to her feet, she slammed the cupboard door. Thank goodness Sara had taken the little ones for a walk. The schoolroom should be empty.

Matty eased the screen door closed and glanced about. Phineas was dumping water into a horse trough, but no one else was in sight. How timely that Mr. and Mrs. Spencer had chosen this evening to visit an ailing neighbor. Matty stole down the garden path and had almost turned the corner when Phineas called.

"Whither thou goest, fair maid?" He hung the bucket by the trough and jogged over to Matty. "Out for an evening stroll?"

Matty froze. After all her talk about not retaliating, what would Phineas think of her plan? After all, he was a boy, too.

Phineas shook his head. "Such a sour look. I'm sorry about this afternoon, Matty. You can borrow the oblique pen whenever you like."

"Thank you," she mumbled, and felt in her pocket for the pepperbox. She had to hurry to the classroom before Sara came back.

Phineas's eyes narrowed. "Hmm, I think there is more on this lady's mind than an evening stroll or a lost pen."

Matty began to march toward the seminary. "There's something I must do," she said.

"What?" Phineas asked. He strode next to her. "Does it have something to do with what's in your pocket?"

"Maybe." She started to jog the last several yards until her hand met the handle of the seminary door. Matty shoved it open and Phineas slipped in after her. His hand grasped her shoulder.

"What are you going to do? Start a bonfire with Jehu's desk? Mr. Spencer would certainly send you home for that prank."

Matty turned around and stared at Phineas. She should have sent him away, but he'd probably have snuck in somehow. And why did his gaze always make her flush? She stuck her hand into her pocket.

"Pepper," Matty said, and brought forth the box. "Red pepper."

"Clever. They won't know until it's too late. But Mr. Spencer will suspect when certain pupils' faces turn red and their eyes water."

"I don't care," Matty said. "I'm tired of them thinking they can tease and torture me. They need to be taught a lesson."

Phineas grinned. "I can't wait until tomorrow morning."

Matty opened the box and set the lid on the first table. Just as she was about to dip into the box, Phineas caught her wrist. "Don't do it to all the gents, Matty. After all, they have done nothing to hurt you."

"Oh, no?" Matty asked. "They haven't tried to stop the others, have they? They sit and snicker along with Caleb and his crew." She bit her lip. She would not cry. She would have justice.

"True. But they are . . . normal boys who think it's fun to tease. And they don't understand why any girl would choose to be here. You're just odd to them." Phineas shook back his hair. "Concentrate on the terrible triumvirate. They are the main culprits."

"Humph," Matty grumbled. She walked over and sprinkled pepper on Caleb's quill and stack of papers. Her heartbeat filled her ears, and her hands were clammy. She hoped no one had seen them enter the seminary. Matty dusted the pepper on Jehu's and Thomas's table.

So the boys thought her odd, did they? She glanced at Phineas. What did he think?

Matty placed the lid on the box and wiped her hands on her apron. She'd wash them properlike back at the kitchen. "I'd best hasten back."

"You go by the road, and I'll slip across the field," Phineas said. "That way no one will see us together. Sweet dreams." He ran out the door laughing.

Matty closed the seminary door and walked home. Tomorrow she would have the last laugh.

The next morning Matty arranged her skirts for the fourth time and adjusted the stones beneath her feet. She dipped her quill and started the exercise yet again.

"Is something wrong, Miss Harris?" Mr. Spencer asked.

"No, sir," Matty stammered. But something would be amiss soon. She glanced at Caleb. He was using the rib of his quill to scratch his ear. He rested his cheek on his hand, pulled it away, and stared at his palm.

Matty looked over at Jehu, who was rubbing his chin and frowning. She bent her head and began to write rapidly. They deserved every second of agony. Somewhere in the room a boy guffawed.

Mr. Spencer wrapped his desk. "Scholars! I've never seen such an agitated lot. What is amiss?"

"I don't know, Mr. Spencer," Jehu said. His eyes were tearing. He rubbed them again, and his whole face turned red. "Something's burning me fierce."

More laughter flew about the room. Matty watched Thomas and Caleb. They were not crying, but their faces were crimson. Phineas winked at her.

"Class!" Mr. Spencer frowned. "You three lads appear to be the victims of some prank. I will not ask the perpetrator to come forward now, but I do expect him to remain after class. I demand an explanation for this disruption. I am weary of all this foolishness."

Matty blanched. Usually Mr. Spencer scolded, but rarely did he keep anyone after class. She'd gone and flung away her future; all on account of those no-good boys. Now Phineas would be in trouble, too. He'd probably never speak to her again.

Mr. Spencer folded his hands and stared at her. Matty looked down at the brown hair on his knuckles and wished she could escape to the apple orchard. How much should she tell him?

"It's my fault, sir," Phineas said. He straightened his shoulders, and his foot kicked Matty's foot.

She jerked her head up. "But I did it, sir," she blurted out.

"I asked her to fetch the pepper," Phineas interrupted.

Mr. Spencer shook his head. "And for what reason did you single out these three particular pupils?" he asked.

"Because they do not like me," Matty exclaimed. "They bumped my paper on purpose, in order to spoil my entry into the contest."

"You know that for certain?" Mr. Spencer asked. He drummed his fingers on his desk.

"Well, no," Matty answered. "But it seemed odd that Jehu tripped right at my desk," she added.

Mr. Spencer sighed. "Miss Harris, I remind you that you are here on probation. School has not been normal since you entered this room. I expect my scholars to be mature individuals who can resolve their differences, real or perceived, in a more mannerly fashion. And above all, a young lady should not debase herself so. If you cannot live up to such standards, then you are not ready to attend this seminary."

"Oh, please, sir," Matty pleaded. "I'll be good, please." She swallowed hard. "Please give me another chance, sir."

"Punish me, sir," Phineas said. "After all, it was my scheme."

"Yes," Mr. Spencer said. "But Miss Harris foolishly acted on it. Consider yourself on probation, too, Master Stewart. You show poor judgment in how to guide a lady. I expect that there will be no more distractions for the rest of this term. You are dismissed." He took off his glasses and massaged his temples.

As they walked down the road, Matty looked over at Phineas, who had stuck a piece of grass in his mouth. "Why did you lie? It was my idea. I did not wish for you to be punished."

"I know." Phineas picked up a rock and threw it at a tree. "But Mr. Spencer reckons boys will pull pranks."

"Humph," Matty snorted.

"I'll catch it tonight from Caleb. Bunking with him this summer has not been pleasant." Phineas tossed another rock. "It would be a pity if you had to leave," he said.

He'd miss her! Dare she tell him that Ma might snatch her away any day soon? It would be a relief to tell someone her secret, to no longer have it knotted inside her.

Matty drew a deep breath. "But I still may be forced to leave." Her palms were clammy, and she wiped them on her apron.

Phineas cocked his head. "Not unless you do not perform well, and you have been practicing, haven't you? Or have you and Sara been too busy chatting?"

Matty grabbed his shirtsleeve. "No, that's not what I meant. It's not like that."

"Well?" Phineas asked. He halted and stared at her. His eyes were like liquid pewter. "Well?" he repeated.

"I ran away," Matty said softly. "Ma wouldn't let me come, so my brother Abe helped me." She could hear his sudden intake of breath. "When Ma finds out . . ."

"She'll come for you," Phineas finished the sentence. "But what if she doesn't find out?"

"Oh, she will! Ma always finds out everything." Matty's knees quaked. "And I must learn enough to qualify as a clerk, for I reckon I can never go back home. She's that angry with me."

Phineas shook his head. "And Mr. Spencer does not know all this?"

"No," Matty stammered. "I was afraid he'd turn me away if he knew that Ma did not send her permission. No one knows. I've kept it a secret."

Phineas whistled. "You've got more grit than even I imagined."

CHAPTER

10

Sara looked up from the tin tubful of dishes and soap-suds. "You look like we've fed you nothing but pickles for a week. And your tone of voice is just as tart."

Matty paused and scowled at the saucer she had dried. "Well, one of us has nothing decent to wear to the Independence Day celebration. While you flounce around in muslin, I'll look like a mossy old oak tree dressed in calico. It would be heavenly to wear a pretty dress."

"What a goose!" Sara retorted. "Do you think, Mama, there might be something Matty's size up in the trunk?"

"There might be, Sara," Mrs. Spencer said. She stacked leftover biscuits on a plate and turned a bowl over them. "You and Matty may look after you finish the dishes." Mrs. Spencer lifted Ellen onto her hip and brushed back the toddler's hair. "I'm going to settle Ellen down for her nap and then sew for a while."

"Let's make haste," Sara said. "I'm sure there is a pink chintz that would fit you." She poured soapy water into a pot and scraped the bottom with a spoon. "There, that's done. I'll go dump the dishwater and rinse this kettle at the pump while you finish redding up."

Matty finished cleaning and set the last plates on a shelf. Housework could be enjoyable when the dishes were beautiful china and there was amiable company. She shook a little basketful of chamomile flowers they had picked and set out to dry. She breathed deeply of the herb's applelike scent. The soothing fragrance matched her mood.

So many mornings had she spent picking the little white flowers for her mother. Ma would just have to do it herself this summer. Chamomile for colic, Ma always said. A shiver ran through her. Only a few more days until Mrs. Chapman's baby was due. Then her mother would know she had run off. How much longer would it be before her mother would discover her whereabouts? And could she trust Phineas with her secret?

"The chamomile is almost dry," Matty said when Sara reappeared.

"We'll take care of that later. Let's go look at the dresses."

They raced up the stairs. A blast of hot air hit them at the top, and Sara pushed open a dormer window for a breeze. "You can smell the honeysuckle all the way up here. Let's shove the trunk into the hallway before we expire from the heat." Together the girls pulled the trunk out from under the eaves, and Sara opened the lid.

"Look at the lace!" Matty exclaimed. She lifted a petticoat and a pair of drawers edged with handknit lace. Her cares seemed to slip through the holes in the eyelets. Matty ran her fingers over the delicate cobweb of linen thread. "Who made these?"

"Aunt Penny. She only has three girls to care for, and they can afford help. So Aunt Penny has time to sew lovely clothes. It seems like I can never find time for such fancywork; all I do is mend for those brothers of mine."

"Has your father convinced your aunt that ovals belong in lace also?" Matty asked. She pointed to the leaves in the design. "And the pointed edges resemble rows of waves." She turned the edging upside down.

Sara laughed. "Papa is passionate about the shapes in nature. I know Aunt Penny has tolerated his lectures over the years, but I doubt if she copied beach pebbles when she knitted this pattern."

"My mother used to knit lace," Matty said. "One time she let me look through a little valise she keeps hidden. In it I found a lace collar she made before she was married."

Sara eyed Matty. "How did your mother come to be a midwife in Michigan? And your father, with so much education. Why did he leave teaching?"

Matty bit her lip and ran the pointed edges of the lace through her fingers. She took a breath and looked up.

"Pa tutored Ma's younger brother, that's how they met. Pa once told me that Ma's father did not approve of him, but they married anyway. I think they eloped."

"Why did they go to Michigan?" Sara held a gown closer to the window, shook her head, and put it aside.

"Because Pa's brother lived there, and Pa thought maybe he could teach in Ann Arbor. When that didn't work out they bought a farm. Sometimes Papa would tutor a few students."

"Was your father experienced in farming?"

Matty shook her head. "No. Papa was a merchant's son and had grown up in town. All my mother knew was how to raise flowers and herbs. I reckon that's why when the farm did not prosper she turned to midwifery. Once she mentioned she had wanted to be a doctor, but she counts that as foolishness now."

"How sad," said Sara. "Your mother must have loved your father very much to leave her home for the Michigan woods."

Matty stared at Sara. "All they ever did was quarrel!" she blurted out. "Oh, Sara, you have no idea what it's like to live in such a horrible home. Pa was always drunk. You are so fortunate! Your parents love each other."

Sara grasped one of Matty's hands. "It hasn't always been so peaceful, Matty. Sometime when you're alone with Mama, ask her about her early years with Papa. I can remember sadder times." Sara took out a dress with pagoda sleeves. The chintz was printed with pink roses.

"Here, this will cheer you up. Why don't you go into our room and try it on?"

Matty peeled off her sweat-soaked calico dress and draped it across her bed. For a moment she held out her arms and felt the breeze cool her body and heart. In her mind she saw herself, six years old and dressed only in her chemise. She had stood in the creek watching shiny minnows dart beside her toes. And then came her mother's voice, scolding her for immodesty. She never could please Ma.

Matty snatched the chintz gown and slipped it over her head. The crisp fabric was cool and smooth with a faint smell of lavender. She twirled around, and the chintz rippled like rose petals falling in a breeze.

Sara peeked through the doorway. "Just lovely," she said. "I'm sure Phineas will ask you to dance with him."

"Sara!" Matty could feel her skin prickle at the mention of Phineas's name. "Just because he talks to me does not mean he favors me. He's only a friend."

"I was merely jesting, but are you certain about that? Most girls would be thrilled to have Phineas's attentions." Sara handed Matty another dress. "Try this frock on, too. Here, I'll help you with the hooks."

"It's so soft," Matty murmured as the gauzelike lawn tumbled about her. The low neckline revealed her collar bones and a slim white neck.

"Stand up straight," Sara said. She fastened the back. "I thought this might be cooler for the afternoon events. This forget-me-not print looks sweet on you." Sara smoothed the skirt and stepped back. "We'll have to sew a few tucks in the skirts of the gowns so they don't drag on the floor."

"Do you really think I should alter two dresses? Will we be able to find the time? We only have three days." Matty held out her skirt and curtsied. Never had she even touched fabric this fine, and now she was clothed in elegance.

"We'll manage. My, you have a little waist. I'm sure someone will want to assist you in a ladies chain." Sara wrapped one arm about Matty's waist and turned her forward.

Matty's feet tangled in the long skirt, and she stumbled. "Sara, stop! I must hem this up before I can dance."

Sara laughed and began to unhook the back of the gown. "Hurry and change, and then you can help me pack away the other things. We should sew in the grape arbor where it's cooler."

The brown calico seemed ordinary as Matty buttoned the front. How wonderful it would be when she could afford lawn. She and Sara pushed the trunk back into place, and, scooping up the dresses, rushed outside.

"The wind feels so good," Sara sighed. She set her sewing basket on the seat. "It certainly was hot upstairs.

Just like the dance hall feels after a couple of long sets."
She glanced at Matty. "Have you done much country
dancing?"

"Only a little. We lived a fair distance from town, and
Ma didn't feel like frolicking much." Matty looked away
from Sara's gaze.

"Most likely there will be a caller to teach you the
steps," Sara said. "But in case there is no caller, maybe I
should show you a few dances. Do you know Petronella
or Sackett's Harbor?"

Matty set aside the dress and faced Sara. "No. What
are the steps?"

"For Petronella you need to balance four times in a
little diamond shape, like this." Sara held Matty's hand.
"Step on your right foot and kick toward the right with
your left foot."

Matty gave a halfhearted kick and giggled.

"Not like that, silly. Put a little bounce into that first
step," Sara said.

"But you look so funny, like you're trying to nudge a
dog out of the way." Matty laughed.

"Well, you could practice on Phebe's banty chickens
over there in Mama's garden. We're always chasing them
out of the flowers." Sara waved her apron and gave a
good kick.

"I'd rather learn how to waltz," Matty said. She
smoothed back her hair and rolled up her long sleeves a
bit. "It's too hot for jumping around."

"Waltzing's easy. Pretend you are a sailboat on Lake Erie's waves, just skimming along." Sara placed her right hand on Matty's waist and grasped Matty's right hand. "Just follow me."

Lilting a tune, Sara guided Matty across the lawn. "You're so light, you float in the air like milkweed down. Just remember to keep your steps even and turn on the last one. There are several other ways to hold your partner. . . ."

"Are there now?" interrupted Phineas, who had appeared from around the side of the house with the twins. "You two make a pretty sight. Your blond and black heads together like that make me think of a goldfinch. A flash of yellow with black wings bobbing along in flight."

Henry and Harvey chortled. "He's as bad as Papa with his poetry," one of the twins said. "Always spouting off some verse."

Matty could feel her face flush. She glanced at Phineas, but quickly looked back at the ground. So he thought her amusing, prancing about the garden! She tried to focus on an ant crawling beside her toes, but her heart was pounding.

Sara glared at the boys. "What are you three doing here anyway? Why aren't you making hay with Papa?"

"What a slave driver," retorted a twin. "We came in for a drink. And it's almost time to milk."

"Oh my goodness," Sara gasped. "We'd better go help Mama with supper, Matty." Hastily Sara gathered up her sewing. "We'll have to sew on these tonight."

"That's right. Make haste," teased a twin. "I'm famished."

Phineas winked at Matty. "Reckon you'll have to learn those other waltz holds at the Fourth of July dance."

CHAPTER

I I

Matty stood brushing her hair. She tried to concentrate on dressing for the Independence Day celebration, but her thoughts kept returning to her mother. By now her mother would have visited the Chapmans'. She gave her hair a vigorous stroke.

Outside the window a flicker drilled into a cottonwood tree. Matty paused and watched the bird. She knew that the long tongue of the flicker would search the fresh hole for insects. Matty's thoughts hammered inside her head to the rhythm of the flicker's beat. . . . Ma knows, Ma knows, Ma knows you ran away.

She threw the hairbrush onto the cherry dressing table and plopped down on her bed. How long before her mother's long tongue would wrap itself around her and, like the flicker, pull her from this place? "I won't go back," Matty said. She fingered the hem of the forget-me-not lawn. "I cannot."

"Cannot do what?" Sara asked. She waltzed into the room and dropped down next to Matty. "Are you worried about the dance tonight?" Sara took a long look at Matty. "Or are you feeling poorly? You look pale."

Matty hid her shaking hands in the folds of her skirt. "I feel fine, just a little worn out from standing next to a hot stove all morning. When do we leave for the celebration?"

"Soon. Mama sent me up to change. Papa went on ahead, but we're all to go in the wagon." Sara pulled the pins from her hair. She combed her hair over her ears and retwisted her braid into a bun. "Is there any water left in the pitcher?"

"It's about half full. Do you mind if I splash a little of your rosewater on my face?" Matty asked.

"Of course not. And there is fuller's earth mixed with rose petals in that little box." Sara nodded to a small oval box. "You'll stay cooler if you dust yourself with it."

Matty slipped the frock over her head, and Sara hooked her up. Matty inhaled and gazed at herself in the looking glass. She felt like a Queen Anne's lace blossom swaying against a blue sky.

Sara lifted the lid from her sewing basket and pulled out a pair of kid slippers. "I hope these fit you." She smiled at Matty.

"Where did you find them?" Matty exclaimed. She slid her feet into the slippers and tied the silk ribbons. All her life she had dreamed of such shoes.

"Aunt Penny sent them, after Mama told her about you." Sara held out Matty's bonnet. "Someone up in Michigan can certainly shape a pretty bonnet. The gray wool makes your eyes seem greener."

"Abe bought this bonnet for me," Matty said. "He gave it to me the day we parted." Matty remembered the feel of Abe's rough woolen vest against her cheek and her brother's strong arms. Abe's clothing always smelled of oxen and damp earth. She bit her lip. It was hard not to miss him.

"I'm sure he will be overjoyed to see you when the summer's over," Sara said. "Think of all that you will have to tell him." She packed the pink chintz and a lavender frock in a basket and tied on her poke bonnet.

Matty stared at the floor. The thought of the summer's end pricked her with fear. She wished she could tell Sara that she could not go home, that coming here had cost her the right to contact her brother. She ran a finger along the grain in the wood of the dresser. If only the summer would never end.

"We'd better scamper," Sara said. "Or the lads will tease us about our vanity."

Outside Phineas gave a low whistle while he helped Matty into the wagon. "The little woodsy blooms as a lady," he whispered.

Matty bowed her head and sat down on the blanket that covered a layer of straw. She hoped no one else had heard Phineas's comment, or they'd be teased.

Dust billowed after the wagon as it lurched down the road. Matty watched the dust cloud roll into the woods and settle on the bracken. The leaves of the sassafras trees hung limply along the few miles to town.

"It's good we're almost there," Sara said after a while. "I don't know what's worse, sitting under the sweltering sun or wiping the grit off my face." She grimaced.

The wagon rumbled around a curve, and Matty spotted the village of Ashtabula. A flock of boys were chasing hoops in front of the schoolhouse, and clusters of women stood in the shade. The young girls' gay frocks splashed color across the deep green of the oak leaves. The twin who was driving guided the horses to a spot near the rear of the school. A volley of musket shots ripped the air, and blue smoke drifted from the gunmen.

Before anyone else, Matty swung herself from the wagon. Her feet itched to run to the bevy of girls. Sara stepped down and handed Matty a basket.

"There are two veterans of the Revolution still alive," Sara explained. "The town salutes them each year. We'd best spread out our quilt. Papa will give his speech soon."

Matty's hands helped Sara smooth out the woolen quilt near a platform, but her eyes followed the crowd. A few of the young women waved at Sara. Off to one side a man with a fife played a reel, and Sara's feet kept time with the tune. This was the largest gathering Matty could remember witnessing, and her own heart seemed to dance to the music.

"Here comes Mama with Phebe," Sara said. "Papa should begin his oration any moment."

Matty spied Mr. Spencer climbing the steps to the small platform. Mothers quieted their children, and men stood still.

"My friends and neighbors," Mr. Spencer began. "Forty-two years ago I stood on the shore of Lake Erie and listened to the cannons roar. I lost two brothers in the War of 1812, but I know they died to secure my liberty and our country's independence.

"And yet my heart remains troubled, and I know that there are others in Ashtabula County who grieve as I do. Not all Americans can claim the same liberty as you and I. For the black man, freedom is but a coveted dream. We must open the hearts of the Southern masters toward their servants. It is a sin to continue the practice of slavery in our dear land, and it must be abolished."

Matty heard a gasp from behind her. "How dare he make such a statement," a woman in a silk bonnet said. "What personal knowledge does he have of our Southern ways?"

"Mr. Spencer's a fine man, ma'am," said a gentleman to the lady. "He speaks from his heart."

From another corner someone cheered, "Hurray for the Master Penman!" Matty glanced about her. Most of the folks seemed to admire Mr. Spencer.

"Another form of slavery abounds in this country!" Mr. Spencer shouted. "The curse of drunkenness ensnares our families. We must free our land from the scourge of liquor!" Mr. Spencer shouted.

"Sign the *T* for temperance," another person cried.

Tears blurred Matty's vision. If only her father had signed a temperance pledge. How different life might have been for her family. She clapped along with the cheering crowd.

"Hope," said Mr. Spencer. "We must cleanse our country of these sins and offer mankind hope." Spreading out his hands, his words rippled across the sea of upturned faces.

> *"Hope is a treasure of the soul,*
> *More clear than all beside.*
> *A voice that ev'ry storm controls*
> *On life's eventful tide.*
>
> *It burns where virtue warms the breast,*
> *As light to realms afar.*
> *Sweet foretaste of unfading rest,*
> *'Tis Hope, our friendly star."*

"Hurray for the Western Bard!" shouted a man.

"Three cheers for our Perrigrine Poet!" said another.

"Are all your father's speeches so passionate?" Matty asked Sara.

"Yes, Papa's been giving speeches since he was four-teen. He's known as a fiery abolitionist and a man of temperance. He allows no liquor near our home," Sara answered. "The crowd usually asks for another poem, but his speech is over."

Mrs. Spencer leaned over. "I think we should go help set up the supper. You know how the men flood toward the food once Papa finishes his last poem."

The girls gathered up the quilt and followed Mrs. Spencer through the crowd. Matty could smell pots of baked beans and the tangy fragrance of salt-rising bread. Her stomach growled. She had never seen such a feast.

Women scurried around the long planks resting on sawhorses that served as a table. Matty and Sara joined the others and set out their pies and crocks of cucumber salad and pickled beets.

"Is this the talented young woman you have told me about?" a stout woman asked Sara.

Sara smiled. "Yes, her only fault is her impatience. She has yet to realize that it takes time to learn a new skill. Matty, I'd like to introduce you to Aunt Penny."

Matty made a little curtsy. "I'm pleased to meet you, ma'am. Thank you for the dresses and the slippers. I've never worn anything so fine in my life."

Aunt Penny cocked her head. She reminded Matty of a ruffled hen. "Such a sweet face you have. I'm glad to see a young lady eager to learn a trade. My brother is right, you know, a practical education prepares you for a successful future."

"You didn't always think Papa was correct in his opinions or his actions," teased Sara. She eyed her aunt and laughed.

"That's true, missy, but if your blessed mother could forgive him, so can I. Now it's about time, Sara, that you found a husband and settled down. Teaching is no substitute for a family," Aunt Penny said, and nodded her head.

Matty watched Aunt Penny walk away. What had Mr. Spencer done that Mrs. Spencer had to forgive?

"Where's the basket with the forks, Matty?" one of the twins asked. Matty spun around and nearly knocked a cherry pie from the twin's grasp. The other twin carried a spice cake, and Phineas held a platter of fried chicken. "And how about a knife, too?"

"Henry and Harvey Spencer!" Sara cried. "Put those dishes down. No one eats until Papa says the blessing."

"Aw, Sara, just let us slip away quietlike. We'll faint if you make us wait until all the grandpas are served. At least let us keep the pie." The twin held it over his head.

Sara giggled. "Here comes Papa now. You three can snack on the pie, but give back the chicken and Aunt Penny's spice cake. You know how Papa relishes it." One of the twins rolled his eyes, and the trio ran for the cover of a clump of lilacs. Sara and Matty turned back and prepared to help serve.

Repeatedly Matty and Sara scuttled between the tables, consolidating dishes and slicing pies. Most of the settlers knew Sara, and some of the young gentlemen lingered.

"Miss Sara, any pie sliced by your hand tastes better," one cocky man said.

Another youth laughed. "And they're even better when you bake them," he added. "And does your sweet friend flavor her cooking as well as you?" He smiled and nodded at Matty.

"She has a lighter hand with the crusts than I," said Sara and placed an arm around Matty. "And have you tried Mrs. Lewis's bread pudding? But really, gentlemen, there appears to be no more space on your plates. Maybe you'd best find a seat."

"We'll just follow you, Miss Sara," one of them said. Plates in hand they joined a few of the local girls and retired to the shade of the oaks. Matty sat on her corner of the quilt, mesmerized by the frolic. Only in her dreams had she imagined so much gaiety and laughter. She nibbled on a chicken wing and eyed the sponge cake on her china plate. Someone squatted down next to her.

"May I join you?" Phineas asked. "You've garnered a ring of admirers I see." He began to search through the clumps of clover.

Matty could feel her neck turn pink. How should she answer him?

"I agree with them entirely," Phineas added, and pulled an exposed ribbon from her slippers, untying the bow.

"Stop it," Matty whispered, and tucked her feet beneath her skirt. She lifted her chin. "It is refreshing not to be constantly teased."

Phineas chuckled. "Make certain you tie those slippers tightly, and I beg that you reserve one of tonight's dances for me." He stood up and shook back his hair. "I have to go practice with the town band now." He dropped something on her plate and walked off.

Matty picked up the four-leaf clover Phineas had dropped and watched him slip into the maze of chattering people.

CHAPTER
12

Several hours later Matty helped Sara stack the last of the Spencer china in a basket along with empty pie plates and platters. Men removed the planking and carried away the sawhorses. The sun had angled behind the trees, and the cardinals sang their evening song. Thank goodness there was still the dance to look forward to.

"We have just enough time to skip over to Aunt Penny's," Sara said. "Aurelia Rose said to come change for the dance with her."

"Where do Aunt Penny and Aurelia Rose live?" Matty asked. "My feet feel like they could fly. I can't wait for the dance." Matty skipped in a circle around Sara. "I hope the night never ends."

"You'll muss your dress with such silliness," Sara scolded. "If you want any partners, you had better settle down. Come now."

The commotion of the picnic faded, and Matty stared at the houses sprinkled along the dirt road. What would it be like to call to a neighbor from your garden? And it must be wonderful to have to walk only a few yards when you needed something from the store. She resumed skipping.

Sara linked her right arm into Matty's left. "See that white house with the picket fence? That's Aunt Penny's. Papa proposed to Mama on the front porch. He met Mama when she was teaching school in town and living with Aunt Penny."

"How romantic," Matty said. She mounted the steps to the porch. A tangle of sweet peas climbed a trellis and scented the air. Sara was right. Aunt Penny must be wealthy to live in such a grand place.

Sara opened the door and glanced at the grandfather clock. "Aurelia Rose! We're here! And we'd best hurry. The dancing commences in an hour." Sara and Matty walked into the kitchen.

"Oh, Cousin Sara," Aurelia Rose said. She stood near a table with a pink rose in her hand. Her image was tripled by the copper pots that hung on the wall, and her pale green dress made her pink skin glow. Aurelia Rose blew her bangs off her forehead. "Don't fret, silly Sara. You know these dances never begin promptly." Aurelia trimmed the stem of a pink rose. "The musicians need time to limber up a bit." She giggled.

Sara frowned. "Papa'd better not catch them."

"You fuss too much, Sara," Aurelia said. "I hope I never become so sour." She tossed her head and led the girls down a hallway paneled in mahogany. Matty gasped when she entered a room even more spacious than Sara's. She curled her toes into the soft Persian carpet and stared at the canopied bed.

"Matty, let me help you with your dress," Aurelia Rose said. She eased the pink chintz over Matty's head and fluffed up the flounce that edged the neckline. "I'm sure the flute player will relish this sweet sight," she said, and pinched Matty's cheek. "I saw him flirting with you at supper."

Matty blushed. Were her feelings that obvious?

Sara rolled her eyes. "If you have not noticed, Aurelia Rose is the dramatic one in the family."

"Such an old maid! You spend too much time trimming quills, Sara," Aurelia Rose retorted. "Have you no memories of your first dance?" She pinned the rose she had trimmed into Matty's hair. "Surely you will blossom tonight."

"Thank you," Matty murmured. Giddy, that's what her mother would have called Aurelia Rose. But Matty wanted to reach out and capture the girl's exuberance. Sara was dear, but tonight she paled in comparison to her cousin.

"What a shy little thing!" Aurelia Rose teased. She grabbed Matty's hands and spun her around.

The music was the first thing Matty noticed when they entered the dance. She stood in the doorway of the school absorbing the rhythms. It was as if the music were an effervescent drink that bubbled inside her and gave her feet a will of their own. She could feel it raise her spirits and quicken her heartbeat.

"Couple up," cried the dance caller. A young man in a blue checked shirt offered his hand, and Matty melted with him into a line of dancers.

"First couples down the outside and up the middle," the dance leader shouted. He loosened his black cravat and jumped up onto a small stool.

Matty felt as if someone had given her wings. She pivoted on the ball of her right foot while her partner swung her around until the room blurred. The pink chintz rippled in a rosy cloud about her and she whirled through the dance as the jigs and reels flowed through her veins. But her eyes skimmed the sea of heads for Phineas's sandy hair.

Matty glanced up as two musicians plus Phineas sauntered through a side door. The cuffs of Phineas's linen shirt were rolled up, exposing his brown arms, and his hair was curled with sweat. One of the musicians cackled and pushed Phineas toward the front of the band.

Phineas tipped his flute toward Matty and her heart lurched. He started a tune, and Matty's partner guided her into the circle of the dance.

"Do-si-do! Balance and swing!" the caller shouted.

Her body had found a language of its own. Matty closed her eyes and let the music command her.

During one of the breaks, Matty fanned herself with her dance card. "Would you like some punch, miss?" one of her partners asked, and handed her a cup.

"Yes, please. My head is still reeling." Matty sipped the punch and eyed the other girls' gowns. Hers was as nice as theirs, maybe even one of the prettiest here. From behind her came Phineas's voice.

"Are you ready to learn those waltz holds?" he asked softly. Phineas set down her cup and placed both hands on her waist. "Put your hands on my shoulders," he commanded.

"Will dancing hurt your leg?" Matty asked. Her heart had risen into her throat, and she could barely breathe.

"Not at all. I'm feeling mighty fine tonight." Phineas laughed and nodded toward the fiddler.

The silver thread of a waltz rippled through the room. Other couples formed and began to glide. Matty tipped back her head and let the breeze fan her cheeks. No motion could be more heavenly than this; even her breathing seemed controlled by the waltz tune. She gasped as Phineas swung her around and around the room. Her feet barely touched the floor.

Matty gazed at Phineas's eyes. They seemed icy and sparkled in an unnatural way. They contained more than his usual teasing look.

"You are smashing tonight," Phineas whispered, leaning closer. He stared at her, and she stiffened. A scent of spirits surrounded him.

"You've been drinking!" Matty whispered. "How could you?"

"Not so loud," Phineas said. He looked about. "Just a nip or two, only to limber up the old fingers."

Limber up? So that's what Aurelia Rose had meant earlier.

"But what about Mr. Spencer?" Matty asked. "You know his feeling toward liquor. If any of his students consumes spirits, he's threatened to expel them."

Phineas shrugged. "As long as you don't tell, he won't know. All the other fellows in the band are from town. They'll keep silent."

Matty released her hold on Phineas. She felt limp and deflated. "You smell like my father," she said, and backed away.

"You won't tell, will you, Matty?" Phineas asked. He caught her hand. "I keep your secret, now you can keep one for me."

"That's not fair!" Matty retorted.

"And why not?" Phineas demanded. "I only took a drink with the fellows."

"You don't understand," Matty cried. "Leave me alone!" She shook herself loose and dashed for the door.

CHAPTER

13

"Matty, is that you?" Sara asked. She peered at the figure huddled in the corner of the wagon. "Is something amiss?"

"The heat made my head swim," Matty said. She wiped her eyes and hoped that sounded convincing. "Has the dance ended yet? I can't wait to go home."

"Almost. They're playing the last waltz. I saw you and Phineas together. He surely could spin you around." Sara leaned back against the wagon. "His flute playing is mortal sweet, just like these stars."

Matty watched a nighthawk soar by and twang its call. Voices and the clatter of boots approached the wagon. Other families placed sleeping children in their buggies and untied their horses. Mrs. Spencer took Ellen from Lyman's shoulder.

"Let me help, Mama," said Sara. She lifted the toddler into the wagon and placed her on a nest of straw. Ellen rolled over and sucked her thumb.

Matty stroked Ellen's head. Teddy sometimes slept like that. For a moment she wished that she could touch Teddy's soft fingers and rub her cheek against his. Matty arranged a shawl over Ellen and avoided Phineas's gaze.

"Phebe's staying with Aunt Penny," said Mrs. Spencer. "And your pa probably will, too. He's off with the historical society."

Matty shifted her skirts so the straw would not prick her ankles. The boys were stretched out at the rear of the wagon and laughter rumbled from their midst. Phineas's voice rose above the others.

"Sara," Matty whispered. She glanced at the boys jostling and pushing each other off the end of the wagon.

"Hmm?" Sara answered, and bent her head close.

"Sara, I'm worried about Phineas." Matty whispered.

"Why? Did you two quarrel? I wondered why you did not stay for the last dance."

"Well, yes, we did, but . . ." Matty paused, her head throbbing. Sara moved closer.

"I fear he was drinking. The band, they kept going outside."

"'Tis their way. Papa should have thought about that possibility before allowing Phineas to join them," Sara said.

"But won't your pa be angry if he finds out?" Matty asked. "Mightn't he expel Phin?"

"Probably not. But he should know about tonight. For his own good, Phineas should not see those fellows again." Sara said.

"Will you tell him?"

"Hmm, why don't you and I talk to Mama first," Sara answered.

"Whoa," called one of the twins. The horses' sides heaved, and the wagon stopped in front of the Spencers' barn. Ellen began to cry and clung to Sara.

"Sara," Mrs. Spencer said. "Could you please put Ellen to bed? Matty and I can tend to the baskets."

Matty touched Sara's shoulder. "But . . ."

"Shh," Sara crooned to Ellen. "Just talk to Mama," Sara whispered. "She'll listen."

Mrs. Spencer placed her baskets on the kitchen table and removed the dirty dishes. "Here, please take these crocks to the springhouse, Matty."

Matty trudged across the yard, opened the springhouse door, and set the crocks inside. Splashing cold water on her face, she closed her eyes and let the water run down her neck. Sara shouldn't have told her to tattle, but if she didn't talk to Mrs. Spencer, Sara would.

Tiptoeing into the kitchen, Matty softly closed the door. "Mrs. Spencer?" she said. "Sara thought I should talk to you, ma'am."

Mrs. Spencer gazed at Matty. "About what, dear?"

"About Phineas. The musicians. They gave him spirits. I smelled rum on him when we danced. He smelled like my father!" Matty began to cry.

"Oh, my dear," Mrs. Spencer said. "Here, we best go into the parlor and talk." She guided Matty down the hall and into a room smelling of leather and beeswax. A patchwork collection of books covered several shelves.

They sat down on a horsehair settee while the faint light of a crescent moon filtered through the muslin curtains. "You were right to tell Sara and me, Matty."

"I don't want Phin to become like my father. Pa was never sober. Never! He could write in five languages, but still no one would hire him."

"Oh, Matty, I could see the sorrow in your eyes. I'm so sorry about your father. Hush now," Mrs. Spencer whispered as she held Matty. "And your poor mother, how she must ache. I know exactly how she feels."

Matty tensed and drew away. "How can you know? You have a husband who adores you. You have no knowledge of what it's like to live with a drunkard. Pa's drinking sucked away all Ma's senses. All she speaks about is marrying me off. She refuses to listen and finds fault with everything I do!"

"Shh. You may think this is heaven, but Mr. Spencer was a drunkard when I married him," Mrs. Spencer began.

Matty gasped. "Mr. Spencer? He never could have been like Pa!"

Mrs. Spencer smiled. "His sister Penny warned me against the marriage. Penny said nothing good would ever come of him and his foolish ideas. But I knew that God was calling me to love Mr. Spencer. And I believed that my prayers and love could cure him of his drinking."

"And did they?" Matty asked. She blew her nose, and tucked her legs underneath her on the settee. Maybe this was the sadness Sara has spoken about.

"Not before I found myself abandoned with three children and living in a log cabin far from town." Mrs. Spencer arose and walked to the window. Her face was serene and strong in the silver light. "I had chosen the cabin because I had hoped that when Mr. Spencer returned from his travels he would think it troublesome to walk nightly to the taverns. But it really was of no matter where we lived, because most often Mr. Spencer was away teaching. I could not accompany him and control his habits. I was forced to teach school to earn enough for our keep."

Mrs. Spencer sat down and took Matty's hands in hers. "And then one spring night God answered my prayers. In fact, I was kneeling and praying when I heard someone shouting for help.

"I snatched the lantern and flung open the door. It had rained all day and melted most of the snow. Mist and fog choked the woods, but I could tell the cries came from Indian Creek. I scrambled through the underbrush, trying to follow the cries. For a second I lost them, and then came a scream. I picked up my skirts and ran."

"Who was it?" Matty asked.

"It was Mr. Spencer! He had fallen off the log bridge and into the flooded stream. In his drunken stupor he was nearly drowned by the current and a tangle of floating branches. When I found him, he was clinging to a bush and couldn't even pull himself out of the water.

"The moment I saw his terrified face, I forgave him of all the past sorrows. I gave him my hand and dragged him out. We walked home together, and with each step Mr. Spencer stood a little bit straighter. He shook himself and squared his shoulders just as we reached our doorsill. And do you know what he did?"

"No, ma'am." Matty wiped her eyes and gazed at Mrs. Spencer's gentle face.

"Mr. Spencer strode to his toolbox, grabbed an auger, and stabbed it into the mantle. He drilled a hole and turned to me and said—"

"'I swear I shall never touch another drop of drink until this hole grow over,'" interrupted the deep voice of Platt Rogers Spencer. Matty jerked around and looked up.

"You rogue," Mrs. Spencer exclaimed, and turned to her husband. "When did you sneak in?"

Mr. Spencer stood barefoot in the doorway. His shirt collar was open, and he held his cravat in his right hand. The candlelight flickered across his face. "And the next day I wrote out my vow of temperance, 'I hereby pledge God and the world that I will never taste another drop of liquor.' I also drew a circle around my farm and promised that drink would never be allowed on my land.

"And if this saint of a woman had not forgiven me and maintained her confidence in me, I do not know what I would be today." Mr. Spencer walked over and stood next to his wife.

"But I don't understand," Matty said. "Why could you forgive Mr. Spencer, but my mother never forgave my father? Do you think she would have forgiven him, if he had given up drink?"

Mrs. Spencer sighed. "I don't know, dear. Her bitterness is just as much a poison as your father's drink.

"Platt Rogers," Mrs. Spencer said. "Matty came to me about Phineas. She said that she smelled spirits on him when he danced with her."

"Phineas?" Mr. Spencer said. "Someone mentioned that the band seemed a little too merry. Phineas played with them tonight, didn't he?"

Mrs. Spencer nodded. "Yes. The musicians are good fellows, but we know that none of them are teetotalers."

Mr. Spencer frowned and gazed at Matty. She shifted her weight and looked down at her hands.

"Did you actually see him imbibing in spirits, Matilda?" Mr. Spencer rubbed his jaw with his fingers.

"No sir, but Phineas acted and smelled like my father." Matty looked away and fingered the edge of her sleeve.

Mr. Spencer sighed. "What a pity. I considered him a trustworthy lad."

"Oh, but, sir, surely he is! It was the band's fault," Matty pleaded. "Being Independence Day and all. Please don't be harsh, sir."

A rooster crowed. "Mrs. Spencer and I will discuss the matter." Mr. Spencer stood up. "And I'll question Phineas in the morning. For now I think we best all try to sleep."

CHAPTER
14

Matty straightened her back but did not stop to check the position of her paper. It had been ten days since the Independence Day celebration, and nothing was going right. Phineas wouldn't speak to her; he just looked away when Matty tried to capture his gaze. Yet she was relieved that he hadn't snitched on her—her secret was still safe.

And lately Sara had been too preoccupied with seminary work to listen to her woes. Sara hadn't even noticed that Phineas was not speaking to her. Maybe Sara never cared to be friends, either. Matty dipped her quill so vigorously into her inkwell that she stuck her finger into the ink. She jerked it out and glared at the other scholars.

Those boys were still like a swarm of pesky mosquitoes, hiding her papers, filling her inkwell with dirt and constantly muttering about her. And she could do nothing about them.

"Miss Harris." She jerked up and looked into Mr. Spencer's face. He had stopped to polish his spectacles. After wiping them, he glanced through the lenses and pulled them on. "Please remain in your seat after class is dismissed," Mr. Spencer said, and gave her a little nod.

"Yes, sir," Matty whispered. Had Phineas told? But why would he have waited to tell? No, it must be something else. Her mother had written. She could feel her hands growing damp. When she dropped them into her lap, a stack of papers slid to the floor. The boy next to her moaned and muttered, "Hopeless, just hopeless."

Tears seeped about her eyelids as Matty knelt to pick up her papers. Hopeless, hopeless. Her mother had used those same words to describe her. Were these boys and her mother right? Was there no hope for her? Was there nothing that she could do right?

Matty plopped into her seat and glanced at the clock. Only thirty minutes left until dinner, and she had five more sheets to copy. She had better hurry. Yesterday she had only been able to turn in half of the work because someone had taken her papers when she went to the outhouse. She had found them later, blown against the rail-fence, and had shown them to Mr. Spencer. He had sighed, shook his head, and said, "Blown out the window again, hmmm . . ."

Steadily Matty copied the exercises, not bothering to wipe dust or lint from her quill. Maybe she could sweeten the scolding if she had all today's work completed.

Sara rang a little bell. "Class dismissed. Whatever is not completed you should finish at home." Matty bit her lip and glanced up. Sara smiled and silently mouthed, "Don't worry." After gathering up a basket of papers to correct, Sara followed the last of the students and quietly shut the door.

While Mr. Spencer stacked papers, Matty swung her legs back and forth, dragging her toes across the floorboards. Mr. Spencer ran his fingers through his hair and looked up. "Matilda Harris, please come and sit nearer." He motioned to a chair in the front of the room.

Oh no, he had used Matilda. Ma must have written. Matty arose and nearly knocked her inkwell off her desk. She marched to the chair and sank into it. She began to play with the edge of her apron.

"How old are you, Miss Harris?" Mr. Spencer asked. "I have forgotten."

"I'll be fifteen, sir, in November," Matty said. Her stomach felt like it had dropped to her toes.

"Fifteen," Mr. Spencer repeated and sighed. "Miss Harris, I want to talk to you about your performance here at the seminary and your future as a penman."

Her heart began to beat more rapidly. Would she have to leave?

"I think you have the talent to be a penman, and I have decided that you may complete the summer term," Mr. Spencer reassured her. "But I am concerned about the quality of your present work. Now, I realize that often you are rushing to redo what others have undone for you." His eyes crinkled.

"Then you know about those boys!" Matty said.

"I've been teaching forty years."

Matty dug her hand into her pocket and concentrated on the roses scattered across her calico dress. If she looked into Mr. Spencer's face again, she knew she'd weep.

His voice was kind. "I do admire your pluck, Miss Harris. Many of my other female students would have given up weeks ago. If the boys had been cruel, I would have intervened, but unfortunately, their attitude is the same one you will have to confront if you ever enter the business world."

She could not squeeze back the tears. They seeped from under her eyelids and trickled down her cheeks. One by one, they dribbled to her chin.

Mr. Spencer walked away from his desk and sat down in the chair next to her. "But the boys are not your greatest problem, Miss Harris. You need more patience. Your work is not of a high enough caliber, at this time, for me to recommend you to a business at the end of the summer. And the reason for the lack of quality is that you hurry through the exercises. You do not strive for flawless perfection by correct paper position or wiping your quill. I know that much of your impatience is derived from the fact that you are eager to learn, to grow up, and to find a job, but first you *must* allow yourself the time to develop a higher level of skills."

Matty stared at the sprigs of roses on her dress growing darker with the steady stream of tears. Never had she dreamed that Mr. Spencer would speak to her so. What would he think if she told him that for her there was only this summer for learning? She would have to find some means of support after the seminary ended.

"So in two or three years you might consider a job as a clerk, but for now, especially since you are so young and a girl, you should consider taking a teaching position. It is obvious that you have a solid education, and what you learn here would give you extra qualifications. Often school boards write me, asking if I could recommend one of my students to them. Please consider this option for the fall," Mr. Spencer said gently.

"Yes, sir," Matty whispered. She rummaged in her pocket for a handkerchief and blew her nose. All she wanted to do was hide, to find a secret place and be alone. She did not want to be a teacher, stuck all day with little boys who threw spit wads and boarding with one family after another in some backwoods county. Even if Mr. Spencer found her a city position, she'd spend all her free time correcting papers. There she'd be, hunched beside a candle, squinting at compositions until all hours of the night, and merely for a pittance.

"For the present, I advise you to slow down. To make each letter deliberately and check those other factors that make for great penmanship. I know you have the soul of a penman, Miss Harris, but for some people, those skills grow more slowly."

Mr. Spencer stood up. "I told Mrs. Spencer not to hold dinner for us, but I do not want her to worry." He gazed down at Matty and patted her shoulder. "And if after a while you'd rather just come in for a cup of tea, I reckon Persis will have the kettle on. She's a remarkable woman." Mr. Spencer set his hat on and walked out the door.

Matty lay her head on the table and sobbed. At least Ma had not found her, but what was she going to do? She had told everyone that she would not even consider teaching! If those boys ever learned about Mr. Spencer's opinion, they'd sink their barbs into her. She could hear them now, commenting on what an eccentric old school-marm she'd become.

After a while her sobs were farther apart and finally ceased. Matty felt like a rose on a bush that had been shaken by a storm and dropped near the ground. Her head hurt, and she rubbed her eyes with her apron. She pushed out her chair and plodded to her desk. She folded her papers and, along with her quills and pebble, shoved them into her apron pocket.

Closing the seminary door, she kicked a small stone as she walked down the lane and toward the orchard. She slipped through the railfence and aimed for a corner far away from the house.

Matty flopped back in the tall grass and watched the cumulus clouds and the waving heads of grass coated with pollen. A few ants and beetles traveled across the highway of green. She breathed deeply. Oh, what a muddle her life was. Was there any way she could change it? The badgering of those boys was a constant distraction for her in the schoolroom. It was difficult to remember all those little details. And then there was the fear that any day would bring a letter from home. She pulled out one of her practice papers. Matty stared at it, blinking back the tears.

She *had* rushed. She usually did have to hurry in order to complete the assignments. Ink had splattered on certain lines, and though the letter shapes grew more uniform near the bottom of the paper, they still lacked that effortless grace. It was as if she had translated the tension of the classroom into jerky lines of letters. Folding the paper certainly did not enhance their appearance, either.

Maybe if she kept her supplies in a basket like Sara did, they would look neater. But how could she improve her lettering? Mr. Spencer was always saying that it took time. It wasn't just that she needed to take more time, but she'd have to make more time. And there was only one way she could figure on gaining that time.

Matty pushed herself out of the grass and slipped around back to the kitchen. All the fellows must be out hoeing corn by now, and Mrs. Spencer was alone. She smiled at Matty. "I saved you a piece of custard pie. Come in and wash your face." Mrs. Spencer went back to kneading bread dough.

Matty lifted the bowl that covered the plate of pie and poured a cup of tea. She sat down at the kitchen table and slowly ate. Mrs. Spencer's deft hands pushed and folded the dough, adding flour now and then. When the dough was soft and smooth, she placed it in a buttered bowl and covered it with a tea towel.

"'Tis amazing how the heat and humidity hasten the bread's rising," Mrs. Spencer said. "Seems like I barely wash the dough from my fingers and the towel is risen over the bowl."

"Yes, ma'am," Matty said, and scraped the last crumbs from her plate. "Mrs. Spencer," she began. "I need help. Most days I cannot finish my assignments during the morning. Somehow I must spend more time practicing. Practicing slowly."

"I know, child. Mr. Spencer told me of your woes," Mrs. Spencer said, and leaned back in her rocker.

"I was wondering if I might try and do more of my housework early in the morning and perhaps save the evenings for practicing?" Matty asked.

Mrs. Spencer stopped rocking and leaned forward. "I'm willing to alter your work schedule," she said, and squeezed one of Matty's hands. "And maybe we can even lighten your load a bit. I'm sure sitting near Sara while she corrects papers will help also. Don't despair, Matty. God will bless your efforts to succeed."

"Thank you, ma'am." Matty squeezed Mrs. Spencer's hand back. How different such kind words made her feel.

CHAPTER
15

꙰

"Scholars, you are dismissed until two o'clock when we will meet in the oat field," Mr. Spencer said, and Sara began wiping the blackboard.

Matty neatly stacked her papers and quills in the basket Sara had lent her. No longer were her papers smudged by her inky fingers nor did they carry as many ink splatters. What was unfinished during class was completed under Sara's patient gaze in the evening.

"Much improved, again, Miss Harris," Mr. Spencer said as she approached the door. "And if you need to leave off shocking oats a bit early this afternoon, you have my blessing."

"Thank you, sir," Matty said, and felt her heart soar. That was the fourth time in the past two weeks that Mr. Spencer had praised her work. Plus he had been working the boys harder on the farm, which lessened their chances for mischief. Matty almost skipped down the road, for even Phineas had flicked a smile at her on his way from the barn. Maybe he had forgiven her. A thread of regret tightened around her heart. Maybe she was the guilty one; after all, Phineas had honored her secret.

Later that afternoon the July sun seared through the hazy sky and beat upon the harvesters. Sweat trickled down Matty's back and a swarm of deerflies circled her sunbonnet. She gathered the bundle of newly cut oats and tied them. Sara worked beside her, and together they built a little teepee out of the sheaves so the grain would dry. They set the last slightly spread-out sheaf on top to protect the teepee from rain.

Matty grabbed another bundle and dropped it instantly. "Oww! There's horse nettles in that one." She tried to flick out the prickers with her thumbnail from her swollen and scratched hand.

Sara stood up and wiped her face with her apron. She glanced at the sun. "In another hour or so Papa might let us go home and start the chores. We could try singing to pass the time. Can you hear Mama?"

Matty listened. From up ahead came Mrs. Spencer's voice.

"Awake my soul, in joyful lays
And sing thy great Redeemer's praise,
He justly claims a song from me,
His loving kindness is so free.

Loving kindness, loving kindness,
His loving kindness changes not."

Mr. Spencer swung his scythe in time with the melody and his voice blended with Mrs. Spencer's. Queen Anne's lace and blue chicory bloomed on the outside of the field, and from one corner a bobolink called.

Matty watched Mrs. Spencer stop for a moment and examine a particular sheaf. "This would be a good one to celebrate the harvest, Platt." She set it aside. "Remind me to bring it to the barn when we go in."

The twins cut the sections on either side of their parents. Their scythes glittered in the sun. A crew of students collected the fallen stalks behind the twins.

"Come now, Matty," Sara said. "I can tell those thunderheads building up to the south are making Papa nervous. He's cutting faster. We need to catch up to Mama."

Matty sighed and stooped over. "Do you think he'll let us rest soon? I need a drink."

"Here comes Phebe now. She's carrying the switchel pail. Somebody's with her." Sara squinted and pushed back her bonnet.

Heat waves rose above the shocks. Phebe trudged toward them while Ellen chased grasshoppers. A man with slicked-back hair and a clean shirt followed behind them. He carried a carpetbag.

"Mr. Spencer," the gentleman called. "Mr. Spencer, please tarry for a moment." The gentleman picked his way across the stubble. His boots were shiny and of thin leather.

Mr. Spencer halted and set down his scythe. He picked up the switchel pail and gulped. After wiping his mouth on his sleeve, he mopped his face with a handkerchief and smiled. "What can I do for you?"

"You are, sir, the great Master Penman, Platt Rogers Spencer?" The gentleman eyed Mr. Spencer's dirty, sweat-soaked shirt and battered straw hat.

"Some call me great. I say I'm blessed. Are you interested in attending my school?" Mr. Spencer asked.

"I?" the man asked. "Oh, no, sir. I've come to challenge you. I traveled from New York City to prove that we on the Eastern coast have refined your offhand flourishing to a new artistic standard." The man opened his carpetbag and lifted out several pieces of penwork.

"He thinks we're all backwoods dunces," hissed one of the boys.

Matty pushed back her sunbonnet and wiped her face. Mr. Spencer would show this outsider that he was the best.

Mr. Spencer thumbed through the papers. "Good work. You should be proud of them."

"Merely good!" the man sputtered. A tic began to twitch by the man's left eye. "I doubt that you are able to produce work better than any of these!"

"If you so desire, I can try," Mr. Spencer said. "Do you have any spare paper?" Mr. Spencer reached for an oat straw from the last swatch he had cut. He pulled a penknife from his pocket and shaped a quill from the straw. He nicked the thumb on his left hand and filled the straw with his own blood.

Oh, no, Matty thought, and watched a drop of blood drip to the ground. Her own thumb ached as if it had been cut. She could feel the bile rising in her throat. "I don't think I can watch this, Sara," she whispered. Her knees felt wobbly, and she squatted down in Sara's shadow. The scene before her seemed to move closer and then move farther away. If she did not watch and breathed deeply, maybe her stomach would settle.

Swiftly Mr. Spencer began to draw. "Unbelievable!" the man gasped. "Amazing! How can you produce such fine flourishes? And you only used a piece of straw and your own blood."

Your own blood throbbed into Matty's mind. The words roared in her ears, and her head spun.

Mr. Spencer handed the gentleman the drawing, and the other students jostled each other for a glimpse of the deep red figure.

Matty turned aside and retched. "Sara, please, help me," she cried.

"Matty! Oh, Matty, you poor thing." Sara knelt beside her. "Mama, please come and help!" Sara wrapped one arm around Matty.

"Not that hopeless girl!" someone said. And then everything went black.

When gray light seeped into her mind, Matty could feel herself being carried.

"In here," Mrs. Spencer said. Strong arms lowered her onto the horsehair settee in the parlor. Through cracked eyelids Matty saw Mr. Spencer running his hands through his hair.

"What a delicate little woman," he remarked. "I suppose my manner was crude. It was that gentleman's tone of voice."

"We all make mistakes, Platt," Mrs. Spencer said. "You leave Matty to Sara and me." She unbuttoned the top buttons on Matty's dress. "Here comes Sara with the rosewater."

"Let me, Mama," Sara said. She wrung out a handkerchief and washed Matty's face. "You can go help Papa finish, while I tend to Matty."

"Thank you, Sara," Mrs. Spencer said, and smoothed Matty's hair away from her face.

Matty turned her head and squeezed back her tears.

"Matty, what is the matter? Do you feel worse?" Sara hovered over her.

"No, I do feel better," Matty answered. "It's just that your mother is so kind and thoughtful. My mother knew that the sight of blood would make me sick, yet she dragged me off to help her at birthings. I'd vomit and faint, and then she'd light into me for being weak and worthless."

Sara continued wiping Matty's face. "I pity your mother, Matty. Certainly all her troubles have created that sternness, and how sad for all of you, but you need to rest. There's a good west breeze to cool you. And if you can't sleep, you could read one of Papa's books."

Matty glanced at the rows of leather-bound books. "The only time I've seen so many books together was in a bookshop in Toledo."

"Well, this is Papa's lending library. He can remember when as a youth he had to walk twenty miles once to borrow a book. So he has these books to lend to neighbors." Sara arranged the handkerchief across Matty's forehead. "I had best go now." She kissed Matty on the cheek and closed the parlor door.

Matty curled up on her side. She had been wrong about Sara; she did care. Sara might not be as exuberant as Aurelia Rose, but she was steadfast. Maybe it was she herself who was fickle.

She stared at the shelves of books. She longed to reach out and caress the soft leather and smell the paper. "Chaucer, Shakespeare, Donne," she read.

"John Donne. Papa used to quote him. . . . 'Go and catch a falling star.' A falling star . . ." Matty's voice trailed off.

She had managed to catch a shooting star when she had entered this home. Sara's friendship and encouragement shone amid the gloom of those boys and the memory of her mother's cutting remarks. Matty closed her eyes. Somehow she must concentrate only on that star and let it light her path.

CHAPTER
16

The sun was setting when Matty awoke. Sara tapped on the door and peeked in. "I brought you some peppermint tea. Would you like it?" Sara glided into the room and set the teacup on a desk. "Mama didn't think you'd feel like supper."

Matty shuddered. To face all those boys around the supper table would be devastating. They'd never let her forget this afternoon. She sat up. "Your mother is so kind, Sara. No, I don't much feel like eating," Matty said. "The tea smells grand."

"I have to hurry back and help Mama." Sara pushed back a few strands of straying hair. "If you feel like it, you might want to practice your penmanship. My grandmother's desk is just your size." Sara pulled out the desk's chair and hurried toward the kitchen.

Matty stretched and walked over to the little desk. It was made from cherry, and the chair seat was covered with needlepoint. Matty ran her fingers across the delicate spindles on the back of the chair and sat down.

Her feet touched the floor! What a pleasant feeling, when something fit just right. She sipped her tea and eyed all the neat pigeonholes and drawers. A few small envelopes perched in one slot. Stacked in a corner of the desk were sheets of linen paper. A glass inkwell rested on a blotter, and several quills lay to one side.

She picked up a turkey feather quill and checked its point, then cast it aside and chose a slender swan's quill. She rubbed its feather along her chin and finally dipped it into the ink. Fifty times she practiced a series of ovals and the other exercises she remembered from this morning's lesson. Her heart sang as her arm fell into the correct rhythm and her pen glided along the paper. It was so much easier to practice without the boys watching her. Finally, Matty wrote out several mottoes:

Fides facit fidem

"Trust makes trust," she translated. Matty wiped her quill and gazed out the window at the orange and lavender sky. Far-off thunder growled. She dipped her quill and said to herself,

Amicus certus in re incerta cernitur

Matty rolled the final *r* in the Latin words. She leaned back in the chair and fingered the pebble she kept in her pocket. She plucked it out and placed it on the desk. A board creaked in the hallway. Matty jerked around and stared at Phineas.

Phineas walked over and looked at her paper. "A friend in need is a friend indeed," he translated. "Your capitals are very pretty. How are you feeling?" He picked up her pebble and rolled it in his palm.

"Much better, thank you." Matty watched the pebble slide through Phineas's slim fingers. She steadied her trembling voice. "Did you finish the oats?"

"Yup. Mr. Spencer even left for Ashtabula, so he can have all day tomorrow to attend to some business. Unfortunately, the horse he wanted to ride was lame, so he took another. He sent me in here for a veterinary manual." Phineas's eyes scanned the bookshelf.

"May I have my pebble back, please?" Matty reached out her hand. She could feel her hands growing moist and her cheeks warm.

"Certainly." Phineas dropped the pebble into her palm. "Did you ever think of how far that stone has traveled?" he asked. "A few ice crystals split it off a granite boulder somewhere. And then it was tossed and rolled along the shores of Lake Erie until the waves ground away the sharp edges. Now you hold a perfect oval."

Matty studied the smooth pink pebble. "Where do you think it came from?"

"Hmm, Canada maybe? All I know is that sometimes I feel like a pebble being crashed about by some wave." Phineas leaned against the doorway and pushed back his hair.

"Matty, I'm sorry about the Fourth of July." He picked up a quill and twirled it around. "I'm not usually like that. Somehow, between the music and the merriment, I lost my senses."

Matty sighed. "What did Mr. Spencer say?" Her chest felt tight.

"I was angry with you for telling, but after Mr. Spencer spoke with me and reassured me that I could stay, I calmed down. I gave him my promise that I wouldn't touch spirits again."

"I'm glad he let you stay," Matty said. "And thank you for not telling him about me running away. You are a more honorable friend than I."

Phineas smiled down at her. He leaned over and sketched a little bird swaying on a stalk of bleeding hearts. Matty could feel the color creep across her cheeks.

"To remember this moment," Phineas said. "And as a promise to you that I will not drink." He set down the quill. "I best go look after Mr. Spencer's horse." He reached up and pulled a thick volume off the bookshelf. "I hope to see you in class in the morning," he said, and walked away.

Matty sat doodling. She eyed the cast-aside turkey quill and started to draw it. From her quill flowed thick and thin lines, while Phineas's words revolved in her mind. When the last rays of light sifted through the trees, Matty laid down her quill and rubbed her eyes.

"How are you feeling, Matty?" Sara asked. She slipped through the doorway and flopped down on the settee. "What a long day! And it's so hot upstairs, I don't know how we'll ever fall asleep."

"I wish the storm would come and cool things down," Matty said. "Is it any cooler outside?"

"A little. Could you manage a walk?" Sara reached for a quill and fanned herself.

"I'd love a walk. In fact, I'm so hot that I wish we could go wading in your creek."

Sara laughed. "It's nearly dark, so Mama probably wouldn't mind. No one would see our legs. Let's go." Sara pulled Matty from her chair. "No time to tarry, or the storm might cool us off."

The girls ran through the orchard, scattering the poultry. The gray geese trotted away, honking and flapping their wings, while all around them cicadas buzzed. Sara pulled an apple from a tree.

"Duchess of Oldenburg. Want a bite?" Sara handed it to Matty.

Matty clutched her skirts in one hand and held onto the apple. For a moment she stood at the edge of the water and then waded in.

"Oh, it's delicious." She closed her eyes and felt the icy water tingle about her shins.

"The apple or the water?" Sara asked. She let something white drop onto the ground and then stepped into the creek.

"Both." Matty squinted at the white heap. "What did you do?"

"Took off my petticoat. Yours is dragging in the water already. Skirts and petticoats are too much to manage on a hot day. I feel cooler already."

Matty traced large ovals in the water with her fingers. "Can you imagine letters this large?" Matty's ovals grew bigger while she spoke.

"I can show you some of Papa's," said Sara. "Once he lettered a twenty-foot campaign banner for President Harrison's election in forty-two. President Harrison was so grateful for Papa's help during the campaign that he offered Papa a job in Washington, D.C."

"And did your father accept?" Matty hitched up her skirts. She could feel the wet cloth hitting her legs.

"No. Papa's a farmer at heart. The banner's in the barn." Sara gazed at the sky. "There might be enough moonlight to see it. That one storm seems to have gone around us."

The girls scampered out of the stream, and Sara slipped into her petticoat. They picked their way through the barnyard and pushed open the small barn door.

Matty inhaled the sweet scent of alfalfa hay. The oxen stood up when the girls entered, and one of them leaned over and rolled his long tongue toward Matty. She stepped back.

"That's Leo," said Sara. "He's always eager for a little extra." Sara scooped up an armful of hay from a pile and gave it to the oxen. "The banner is in the loft." Thunder echoed far away, and heat lightning flickered across the sky.

Sara scrambled up a ladder, and Matty followed. "Over here, by this window," Sara said. She lifted a large bundle off a shelf and began to unroll the cloth.

Matty read aloud, "'William H. Harrison, His Conscience Keepers Are Patriotism, Honesty, and Ability.' How did your father use this?"

"I think during an Independence Day celebration. I wasn't very old, but I remember Papa making a speech." Sara began to roll up the linen banner.

Matty glanced around the barn. The loft was half full of hay, and on the walls hung birdhouse gourds, old baskets, and a few pitchforks. A gust of wind rattled a large barn door below. She shivered and pointed toward a door in one wall. "Does the door lead into the other wing?"

"Haven't you seen all the barn yet?" Sara asked. "Might as well go have a look." She paused at the door.

Matty stared at Sara. "I hear voices," she whispered.

Sara nodded her head. "Somebody's in there. It could just be the twins." She eased open the door. The girls squeezed through and halted.

Below them at ground level stood the musicians who had played at the dance and several seminary scholars. A lantern sat on a crate and cast a circle of light. Several students lounged about, and a tin cup was being passed.

"How are you going to make it down?" said one musician. He leaned back and stared upward.

Matty looked in the direction of the musician's eyes and saw Phineas. He stood on the uppermost beam, even higher than the loft, holding a sheaf of wheat.

"Sara, he's going to kill himself," Matty whispered. "That must be liquor in their cup." Her lungs felt like they were collapsing, and she leaned against the door.

Sara squeezed Matty's shoulder. "Hush. Don't startle him."

Phineas inched his way along the overhead beam. Stopping in the center, he pulled a hammer from behind his suspenders and whacked a nail into the beam. At last he hung the sheaf on the nail.

"Hurray for Phineas!" shouted one of the students.

"Harvest Home!" another cried.

"He still has to climb down," jeered a musician.

The girls crept closer to the loft's edge. Matty wiped her sweaty palms on her dress. Oh, Phineas, don't look down, she prayed.

Phineas pulled himself along the hand-hewn beam. Matty could see his jaw muscles working, and sweat trickled down his forehead. He paused where the roof rafters rested on the header, slid his feet onto the angle brace, and began to let himself down. His feet reached out and searched for a foothold on the upright beam. Suddenly his hands slipped and he screamed.

"Phineas!" Matty shrieked. She winced as his head struck the angle brace, and she ran to the beam. Phineas dangled by his suspenders at the loft's edge.

Matty grabbed at him, unaware of Sara's firm grasp on her waist, and together they dragged Phineas onto the loft. Matty wiped the blood and dirt away from the cut on Phineas's forehead.

"Sara, he's bleeding," she said, and swallowed hard to force the nausea down. Her ears filled with roaring, and she shook her head. She couldn't be sick again. "We must carry him to the house." Footsteps thundered around her and mingled with the coming storm. She must only think about how he needed her help, Matty told herself, and slowly her head cleared.

"Find a board!" Matty shouted to the boys. Someone scrambled over to a lumber pile. Matty watched Phineas breathe and mopped his face. Tenderly she helped the boys ease Phineas onto the board. They lifted the stretcher and started down the loft ladder.

Phineas groaned. He opened his eyes and squinted up at her. "Matty?"

She leaned over. "You fell. We're taking you to the house." Matty flung herself down the ladder and raced to the garden. Lightning lit her way, and the first big raindrops splattered across her face. She stopped at the comfrey plants and ripped the prickly, broad leaves from their thick stems. She dashed toward the house with her arms full of leaves. "Mrs. Spencer," she shouted. "Help! Phineas is hurt!"

Mrs. Spencer ran to the doorway and held a candle-stick aloft. "This poor lad seems to have a penchant for scrapes. Take him to the parlor. What happened, Sara?"

"He fell off a beam in the barn. His suspenders snagged on a nail. Matty and I rescued him." Sara pumped water at the sink. "I think it was a dare, Mama."

"I picked some comfrey," Matty said. Her hair had come unpinned and tumbled down her back. "We should poultice the cut with fresh leaves."

"Bless you, child," Mrs. Spencer said. "Let me stir up the fire in the stove." She glanced at the dripping huddle of boys. "Since the storm has abated for the moment, I think you had best retire, gentlemen."

The boys mumbled their parting and tramped away.

Sara chuckled. "What a lot of scamps!"

Matty turned to the table. "Scamps is too good a word to describe that bunch." She began to crush the comfrey with a knife. "Here, when the water is hot, steep these leaves for five minutes," she explained to Sara. Matty wrapped the remaining crushed leaves in a napkin and hastened after Mrs. Spencer.

Cushioned by quilts, Phineas lay on the floor. Mrs. Spencer sat next to him, moving his legs. The candles flickered as rain beat against the windows, and thunder rattled the panes.

"You're fortunate that you did not rebreak that leg," Mrs. Spencer remarked. "You're just bruised up a bit." She arose. "Here comes your guardian angel."

Matty knelt down and laid the poultice across Phineas's forehead. His face was no longer pale, and the blood was clotting. Her hair brushed his cheek. Phineas reached up and grasped her hand. Her own hand seemed so small in his broad palm.

"Maximas gratias, amicus certus?" he whispered. Phineas's eyes questioned hers.

Matty smiled and squeezed his hand. "Sure friends," she murmured.

CHAPTER

17

A screech owl wailed in the early morning, and Matty rolled over. Sara slept deeply, but Matty eyed the piles of crumpled dresses flung across a chair. The muddy petticoats and blood-stained skirts verified that last night had happened.

Matty slipped from the bed and donned her clothes. Fog beaded the cheesecloth screen tacked over the window frames. The screech owl's call rolled down the scale, and Matty descended the stairs. The pebble in her pocket bounced against her thigh, and instinctively Matty reached in and held it.

"Good morning, Matty," Mrs. Spencer said. She sat holding a cup of tea with both hands. "You're an early riser."

"I couldn't sleep." Matty ran her fingers back and forth along the top edge of a chair. She glanced at Mrs. Spencer. "How's Phineas?"

"He had a restless night. His head still hurts, and he's a little dizzy."

"Mrs. Spencer," Matty said. "Do you think he was drinking spirits?" She continued to run her fingers across the spindles of the chair.

"Why don't you ask Phineas yourself?" Mrs. Spencer poured two cups of tea. "He's still in the parlor. You can take tea and toast to him. That way I can begin breakfast." Mrs. Spencer smiled and gave Matty a tray.

Phineas lay on his pallet on the floor. With one finger he traced around the shapes of a quilt block. He eased himself up when Matty entered.

"Matty, you're too good to a wayward fellow like myself!"

"How are you feeling?" Matty asked. She handed Phineas his tea and sat down at the little desk.

"Better, thank you." Phineas shifted his weight and winced. He drank his tea and bit into the toast.

Matty's hands shook while she collected her practice papers from last night and stacked them in a neat pile. At last she took a deep breath. "Phineas, what possessed you to take such a risk? You could have been killed! And now, Mr. Spencer will have to expel you for drinking spirits."

Phineas put down his toast and stared at her. "I kept my promise, Matty. I did not drink. Do you still not trust my word? I thought those fellows came to play music, but they meant to make trouble. It was after I refused their rum, that they proposed their dare to hang the harvest sheaf from the upper beam. They kept teasing me and telling me I was worthless." Phineas sighed and leaned his head against the settee. "That penmen aren't manly because we work at desks."

"Oh, Phineas." Matty shook her head. "Why didn't you point out that Mr. Spencer's a farmer? He can probably plow more acres in a day than any of those boys. And he's the greatest penman in America."

Phineas scowled. "They weren't attacking Mr. Spencer's abilities, and I do have my honor. Which is something you do not seem to understand. I twice gave you my word, and neither time have you trusted me."

Matty stared at the empty teacup. He was right. He had kept his promise not to tell her secret, and now he had kept his word about spirits. "I'm sorry, Phineas," she whispered. "I did not mean to question your honor." She tucked her papers into her apron pocket. "I had best go help with breakfast," she said, and fled the parlor.

Back in the kitchen Matty flipped pancakes and heaped them on a large platter. What sort of friend was she that she kept questioning Phineas's word?

The kitchen door slammed. Sara stumbled in and set down a bushel of cucumbers. "There's our work for the morning. With all the heat the pickles grew faster than I reckoned."

After breakfast the misty gray morning hours fell away like the cucumber slices Matty and Sara chopped.

Together they worked at the kitchen table layering the pickles into crocks. Into another crock they jumbled various garden vegetables and over all the mixtures they poured a salty brine.

"There," Sara said. "It's so satisfying to see the pantry fill up with crocks and jars." She wiped her hands on her apron. "Why don't you go and read to Phineas? He's still in the parlor and probably yearning for company."

Matty found him waving one arm and quoting Shakespeare.

"To-morrow and to-morrow and to-morrow,
Creeps in this petty pace from day to day"

Matty laughed and startled Phineas. "Your head must be feeling better." She gave him a shy look. "Would you like me to read to you? Maybe you'd like the passage about Patience and Passion from *Pilgrim's Progress?*"

Phineas chuckled. "Next you'll be saying that I need to hear about the 'Valley of Humiliation.' Well, read on, please." He squirmed about on the settee.

Matty selected *Pilgrim's Progress* and began to read. Now and then she swatted at a fly and paused to turn the pages. Both she and Phineas jumped when they heard the familiar boots of Mr. Spencer stepping down the hall.

Phineas froze. Matty's voice caught in her throat. What would Mr. Spencer say to Phineas after last night? She rose from the chair and stood clutching the book. Mr. Spencer walked toward her.

"Miss Harris," he said. "A letter has arrived for you." He held out the slim envelope with a crescent moon postmark.

Matty cringed. The postmark of her hometown blazed up at her. Ma had found her. The only time in her life she had received a letter, and it had to come from her mother.

"No," she cried and stepped back. "I won't take it. Please don't make me."

If she read it, she would have to leave, Matty thought. Everything would end. Mr. Spencer would never allow her to stay once he knew her secret.

"Take it, my child." Mr. Spencer reached for her free hand and pressed the letter into it. "You know it must be important."

Matty stuffed the letter in her pocket. She flung down the book and dashed out of the parlor. The kitchen door slammed behind her, and Matty ran across the barnyard. She slipped between the split rails and headed through the pasture and toward Lake Erie.

Matty could hear the thunder of the waves. At the top of the small cliff, the northwest wind snatched away her breath. She plunged downward, sliding on the fragments of shale. Matty paused when she reached the base of the cliff and pulled the letter from her pocket. She stared at the handwriting.

Her mind whirled. The address was written in Abe's firm hand and not her mother's. Aloud she read:

My dearest sister Matty,

Each morning I have prayed for you and longed to know if you were safe at Mr. Spencer's school. I hope these weeks of instruction have brought you closer to your dream of being a penman.

Ma did not learn of your absence until she attended Mrs. Chapman. Ma was oddly calm about your departure. I think her mind was ailing. She was struck by fever the next day.

Matty turned the letter and read the crosshatched lines.

Little sister, we need you here. Ma has been bedridden for a month. I cannot cope with the harvest and nurse her. Teddy also has been ill.

Please come home. It grieves me to ask you to leave your studies, but I see no other way to manage. I am sending all the cash I have. Hopefully you can borrow the remaining fare.

May the Lord shield you and speed your homeward journey. I remain your loving brother,

Abram Harris.

Matty tucked the letter back into her pocket and walked down to the beach. The foaming breakers towered above her. They crashed against the strand, scattering pebbles up to the base of the small cliff. She stared at the bubbling green water. Mountains of whitecaps could be seen far out into the vast lake.

She felt a tug at her ankles as the fingers of a wave spread out across the beach. A haphazard trail of stones marked how far the wave had flowed. Matty glanced at the rocks. They were mostly ovals.

What was it that Phineas had said? That in a way we are all a little like a pebble battered about by the waves. She certainly felt like a pebble caught up in overwhelming waves of troubles. Sorrow had seeped into the marrow of her bones. A piece of paper with a few pen strokes had swept away her dreams. Even teaching school somewhere would offer more opportunities than going back home to Ma. But how could she disappoint Abe?

There was no hope for her. No matter how hard she tried, there were always problems to stop her. Matty clenched her teeth and pulled her pebble from her pocket. Stupid pebble. She didn't need it reminding her of what she could never be.

Matty stepped forward and raised her arm. A large wave unexpectedly crashed against her shins and sucked the sand from beneath her feet. She stumbled backward and stood sobbing.

Her tears wet the pebble, and the mica sparkled at her from its background of pink and white. It had glittered like that when Mr. Spencer first placed it in her hand. So many times she had stared at this pebble, engraving its oval shape on her mind. Only after she could see the shape could she write her letters, her beloved, beautiful letters. Matty pressed the cool rock against her cheek.

"'The most perfect shape in nature,'" she quoted. She gazed out across the lake until the constant motion of the water calmed her, and her breathing fell into the rhythm of the waves. After all, Abe had said he needed her now, but maybe in a few months . . . Matty slipped her pebble into her pocket.

"Matty," Sara gasped. She ran up and grabbed Matty's hand. "Are you all right? Papa said you received a letter that troubled you."

"Yes," Matty said, and wiped sand from her hands. "I must go home."

"Why?" Sara asked.

"My mother and Teddy are sick, and Abe needs my help." Matty dug a little hole in the sand with her toe. "But after being here, it will be so hard to go back to Ma."

Sara took Matty's hand. "Perhaps your mother will think differently when she sees all that you have learned."

Matty shook her head. "You don't know Ma. But I guess it's like Pa used to say, '*Omne initium est difficile.*' Every beginning is difficult."

CHAPTER
18

Matty watched Mr. Spencer's boots pace back and forth across the kitchen floor. Their scuffed toes matched the well-worn pine boards. Outside a cardinal gave its chipping evening call. Mr. Spencer cleared his throat.

"I've often pondered why it is my most talented students who fall into so many scrapes. I suppose it's the artistic passion erupting along the wrong course." He pulled out a chair and sat down. "Hopefully Phineas has learned to master his will after his daring adventure."

Matty glanced up at Phineas. He sat opposite her at the kitchen table.

"I think I have, sir," said Phineas. "And I promise in the future to remove myself from any questionable gathering. I'll be a different man in Pittsburgh."

Pittsburgh? Matty looked over at Sara who was piecing a quilt block, but Sara just smiled.

"Matty," Mr. Spencer said. "I've asked Phineas and Sara to assist me at the Spencerian Business College in Pittsburgh this fall. Sara had suggested that you come along and help her. I thought that under her gentle guidance you might have gained the skills to qualify for a job as a junior clerk. But of course, your sudden news alters that plan."

Matty turned pale. To live in a city, to browse in bookstores, to spend each and every day with Sara and Phineas in the world she longed for. They wanted to share it all with her. But none of this was to be. It hurt to breathe. Slowly she drew out her words.

"I have to go home, sir. My brother needs me." Matty tried to squeeze back the tears, but they tumbled forth. "And he's always been so good to me, sir, stepping in to be a father when Pa couldn't."

Mrs. Spencer set down the sock she was knitting and put an arm around Matty. "You are right to go home, my dear. God will bless you for your sacrifice."

"But I don't want to go home!" Matty cried.

Mrs. Spencer hugged Matty. "One day you will realize that you acted in the correct manner."

"We were hoping," said Mr. Spencer, "that, after your mother recovers and the crops are harvested, your brother might send you back to us." Phineas raised his eyebrows and looked at Matty.

Matty drew in her breath and let it out slowly. There was still hope. "I will have to wait and answer after I speak with Abe, sir," she said. "But you know I want to say yes." Matty felt for the pebble in her pocket and made a wish that her mother would recover quickly.

"And now we need a way to send you home," Mr. Spencer said. "We could lend you the remaining funds needed for the train fare, but I have an idea. And it may be just the arrangement to help out another friend in need. You will have to hurry and pack. You'll depart in the morning."

Late that evening Matty stood in her room and packed her few frocks in her basket. She turned around in her hand a teacup sprinkled with pink flowers that Mrs. Spencer had given her. Because of such kindness she would drink tea from china at home.

The call of a whippoorwill floated in the open window. The bird seemed to mock her, "Penman girl! Penman girl!" Someday maybe, if she kept practicing. Matty wandered over to the dresser and pulled out her dancing slippers. She could hear Sara climbing the stairs.

Sara walked in and held out a large bundle. "Mama and I want you to take this fabric. There's several yards. You might even squeeze out a new sunbonnet."

Matty stroked the creamy calico sprinkled with lilacs. Lilacs were her mother's favorite flowers. "Oh, thank you, Sara. I'll be thinking of you as I sew each stitch."

"I also made this for you," Sara said and slipped a little packet in Matty's hand.

Matty opened it and recognized the quilt block Sara had been sewing. Across a muslin square was penned:

May the joys of your life be many
May the griefs of your life be few,
May your trust be in Him
Who will safely carry you through.

"It's beautiful, Sara, thank you. When did you find the time to finish it? And you used scraps from the dresses we wore to the Fourth of July dance!" Matty reached out and squeezed Sara's hand.

"I wanted you to have a friendship block. I started an album quilt with a few friends back in Pittsburgh. I do hope you join us this winter, Matty. Remember to save the scraps from the calico for a quilt of your own."

Matty hugged Sara. Something rattled against the wall of the house. She and Sara stared at each other. More gravel hit the house, just above their window. Matty peered into the darkness. Below Phineas motioned to her.

"Meet me in the parlor," he said softly.

"Why?" Matty shook her head. "You should be resting."

"Come, please," Phineas pleaded.

"Allow him a brief moment," Sara suggested, and gave Matty a gentle shove.

Downstairs, Matty pushed open the parlor door. Her hands shook and her heart fluttered. Phineas stood by

the bookshelf, and his hair seemed silver in the moonlight. He offered her something.

"I wanted to give you this when we were alone."

Matty stepped to a window and held the paper in a
shaft of light. Her eyes widened. "Phineas, it's magnif-
icent. You can flourish almost as well as Mr. Spencer.
I've never seen such delicate ferns and little birds."

"Read what it says," he whispered.

Accept my friend this little pledge
Your love and friendship to engage
If ere we should be called to part
Let this be settled in your heart
That when this little piece you see
You ever will remember me."

"Thank you, Phineas," Matty murmured. The
moonlight seemed to shimmer inside her and made her
heart glow.

Phineas took one of her hands. "You will join us in
Pittsburgh, won't you, Matty?"

Matty's hand tingled at his touch. She looked out at the moon. "I can't promise now, Phineas. I will have to discuss the matter with my brother."

"May I at least write to you?" he asked.

Matty turned and smiled into Phineas's pleading face. She hoped she would see it again soon. "Yes, you may write me." She withdrew her hand and started to leave.

"Please," he said, "write a bit in my autograph album. I left it on the desk." Phineas pulled out the little chair and lit a candle.

Matty sat down and picked up the swan's quill. She opened the little book at the back and wrote:

Amicus animae dimidium

"'A friend is a half of one's soul,'" translated Phineas. "Thank you, dear Matty!" He lifted the book and blew on the paper to help the ink dry.

"I won't be able to see you in the morning," he said. His jaw muscles twitched. "Mr. Spencer asked me to help Sara since he will be taking you to town." Phineas closed the album and looked down at Matty. Gently he moved a strand of hair away from her eyes. His fingers brushed her cheek, and Matty trembled. "May God watch over you until we meet again."

"*Vale,*" Matty whispered, and slipped from the room.

• • •

Early the next morning Matty walked toward the waiting wagon. One of the twins stood nearby and lifted her basket into the wagon. He winked at her as he slipped one of the funny oblique penholders into the basket.

He leaned over. "I'm Harvey, and I wanted you to have one of my pens. You were a good sport, Matty."

"Thank you, Harvey," Matty said. "I am honored by your gift, and I'll always think of you when I write with it."

"I've a note for you, too," Harvey said. He handed Matty a slip of paper, and she opened it.

Matty's eyes widened and she sucked in her breath. Caleb's signature was at the bottom of the note! She scanned the words.

> *I still don't think girls should be penmen, but you were decent about the teasing. And you were brave when you saved Phin. For a girl, you aren't a bad penman. Caleb*

"I think he wanted to apologize," Harvey mumbled. He looked down at his boots and then up at her. "Any return messages?"

Matty sighed. After all the trouble Caleb and his crew created for her, and now this. There was no doubt that they'd all find jobs as penmen, while she might rot at home forever.

"Oh, tell them they're forgiven," she said and stuffed the note into her pocket. At least he had said she was a decent penman.

Harvey helped her into the wagon and tucked in the lap robe. The horses shook their manes when Mr. Spencer climbed in and slapped the reins. They were off toward town.

Mr. Spencer was silent as they rolled toward Ashtabula. Sometimes his lips twitched with a smile. Matty gazed upward at the intense blue sky. A few cumulus clouds floated overhead, and crickets chirped. Along the roadside wild hop vines bloomed.

Suddenly Mr. Spencer began to speak:

> *"I seized the forms I loved so well*
> *Compounded them as meaning signs,*
> *And to the music of the swell,*
> *Blent them with undulating vines."*

He nodded toward the vines. "Hops is one vine that is hard to weed out. Would you like me to say the next stanza?"

Matty smiled. "I'd love to hear it and any others, sir." Anything to distract her mind from thinking about Ma. And how did Mr. Spencer plan to send her home?

Mr. Spencer recited on, and soon they were parked at the Ashtabula wharf. Matty glanced about. Was he sending her by boat? She followed Mr. Spencer down the pier where he stopped in front of a large sailing ship. There were barrels and crates stacked up and down the pier, and sailors were racing back and forth loading the ship.

A stocky man with a beard stood next to the gang-plank and was shouting orders. He spied Mr. Spencer and Matty. "Where's the lad you promised me, Platt?" he asked.

Matty's eyes darted from Mr. Spencer to the captain. Her stomach churned. Had Mr. Spencer tried to trick this man? Her body froze as the truth permeated her mind.

"I did bring you help, Amos. I didn't promise you a lad. I promised you one of my best students." Mr. Spencer placed a hand on Matty's shoulder. "The boy Phineas had an accident and could not come, but I think Matty will do a fine job. She's a hard worker and is in need of passage back to Michigan."

Matty felt her blood stir, and her heart beat rapidly. Mr. Spencer was recommending her for a job, and he had praised her in front of this man!

"A girl! And just a little slip of a thing at that! I bet her feet don't even touch the floor when she sits down." Captain Amos frowned.

Matty breathed deeply and looked at the captain. She stepped closer and her voice rose firm.

"I'll do my best, sir. I may not be big, but I'm persistent."

Mr. Spencer laughed. "She's a rare one, Amos. Are you sure you don't want her help? She'll speed your voyage along, and she needs to return home to nurse her mother."

"I should have known you'd play one of your tricks, Platt," said Captain Amos. "You deserve those scamps you call sons." He looked down at Matty.

"All right. I'm in too much of a bind to say no. My clerk insists that he cannot handle the accounts alone. Never seen so much cargo being shipped to Detroit. My missus and young'un are along, so maybe you can lend a hand there as well."

"Oh, thank you, sir. And thank you, too, Mr. Spencer." Matty shook his hand. "Thank you for each golden moment of this summer."

"God bless you, Matty. And once you reach Detroit, the funds Abe sent should pay for your train ticket back home," Mr. Spencer said.

He headed toward the wagon and Matty climbed on board. She gazed over the marsh that hugged the bay. The lowlands were dotted with clouds of white flowers.

"Boneset," Matty murmured. "That's just what Mama and Teddy need. I'll have to brew them some tonic when I get home." She reached down for her basket and cried out, for underneath the railing were the initials:

"This is the ship Mr. Spencer clerked on!" Matty exclaimed. She stared at the graceful letters. Matty felt in

her pocket and pulled out a pencil stub and inscribed her
own initials.

"My capitals are almost as good as those Mr. Spencer
could make back then," she whispered. "And if I keep
practicing, someday I might be a master penman, too."
She looked up at the billowing sails as the ship began to
move. Even if she was homeward bound, the present
days would be as full as the sails overhead. She was
working as a penman before any of those vexing boys.

Someone chuckled, and Matty jumped up. It was a
young woman holding a baby. She pointed toward a set
of stairs. "I just heard about you. The clerk's office is
below. And when you feel like some female companion-
ship, come and have tea. Lovely letters," she added, and
nodded toward Matty's initials.

"Thank you, ma'am," Matty said, and smiled at the
lady. She straightened her shoulders and picked up her
basket. It was time to set to work with her pen.

CHAPTER

19

"Thank you, Mrs. Byrd," Matty said, and set down her teacup. "I've relished these afternoon teas spent with you." She glanced about the captain's quarters. It was paneled in chestnut, and a kerosene lamp with a green glass shade swung from the ceiling. A large oriental rug covered the polished floor. The room seemed to demand that she sit up ramrod straight.

Mrs. Byrd smiled and passed a plate of cookies to Matty. "Your company has been a special blessing on this trip. I certainly admire your pluck, Matty. You see, when I was your age, I longed to go to sea."

Matty looked up from the cookies. Clothed in gray silk and lace, nothing in Mrs. Byrd's manner hinted of the seafaring spirit.

"But such occupations are not suitable for ladies," Mrs. Byrd said, and sighed. "I have always been grateful that the good Lord gave me a sea captain for a husband,

and one who enjoys the presence of his wife on shorter voyages." Mrs. Byrd refilled Matty's teacup and handed her the cream pitcher.

"Captain Byrd is a generous man, ma'am." Matty said. She stirred her tea with a silver spoon and watched the cream swirl.

"I guess time and motherhood fade such silly notions," Mrs. Byrd said. "I can't imagine any task more satisfying than caring for my little angel." She gazed at her young son sleeping in his cradle. The clock on the wall struck five o'clock.

Matty swallowed the last of her tea. "I best be off, ma'am. Mr. O'Dowd told me he had several more papers I must copy before we arrive in Detroit tomorrow." Matty arose and held out her hand. "Thank you again, ma'am, for all your kindness. You are a true lady."

Mrs. Byrd pushed back her chair and hugged Matty. "May God bless you, my dear, both as a penman and on your homeward travels."

Mr. O'Dowd looked down his long nose at her. "You are tardy by three minutes, Miss Harris. I requested that you return by five o'clock." He scowled. "Fine penman you'll make with such slothful habits. If you enjoy drinking tea so much, maybe you should reconsider your aspirations."

"Mrs. Byrd and I were saying farewell, sir," Matty answered, and sat down at her desk. "It's doubtful if we shall see each other again. I assume that tomorrow we will be busy until all the cargo is unloaded, and by that time Mrs. Byrd will be visiting her sister."

"You certainly shall be busy," Mr. O'Dowd said. "Clerks are usually the last to leave ship." He slammed a ledger closed and handed a large stack of papers to Matty. "I will examine your work after I have had my dinner. And, Miss Harris, if you wish to succeed as a penman, you should learn to hold your tongue." He shoved a hat on his bald head and strode out the door.

Matty glared at Mr. O'Dowd's back and checked her impulse to stick out her tongue. He was such a crotchety character. An afternoon tea party would do him good.

Matty laid down her quill. Only a few more days and she must face Ma. Fear clutched her stomach. Seeing Abe and Teddy again would be mortal sweet, but Ma. How would she ever manage to cope with Ma again? Even with all the boys' teasings to withstand, she had felt alive and hopeful at the Spencers'. Matty bit her lip and dipped her quill. That stack of records would demand an hour or more of labor.

Later that evening Matty looked up at Mr. O'Dowd. His mouth was a thin line in his round face. "These two have ink spattered on them, Miss Harris. I realize in your inexperience that you will make mistakes, but you should never turn in such work. Recopy them until they are perfect." He let them flutter onto her desk. "And if you find that thought disagreeable, then find a job more suitable for the weaker sex." Matty's shoulders drooped as she watched Mr. O'Dowd exit.

She turned and lit the kerosene lamp mounted on the cabin wall. Her eyes hurt, and there was a kink in her neck. She laid the two papers in front of her. It was not fair that Mr. O'Dowd said she had to make them perfect. Matty scowled. She had seen when he had spattered ink on his work. Was it always going to be this way? Would more be required of her than the male clerks? At least Captain Byrd had praised her performance on the voyage.

She rubbed her eyes. Sometimes clerking was even harder than housework. It was difficult to sit still all day. And she never had been very good with figures, but still she loved the smell of the ink and the way letters flowed from her new pen.

She laid her head down on her arms. What were Phineas and Sara doing tonight? Were they making plans for Pittsburgh?

Matty jerked up. The ship had stopped rolling, and outside her window winked a few lights. She could hear the hoofbeat of horses on cobblestones. She squinted at the clock. She had slept three hours, and there was still one errant paper unfinished.

She sighed and dipped her quill. She'd not give Mr. O'Dowd any more reasons to fault her work.

CHAPTER

20

Matty slowed her steps as the trace twisted toward her home. Just as the railroad had quickly taken Matty to Ashtabula, another train had swiftly returned her to her hometown. A few more yards along this path would bring the clearing into sight. Matty shifted her basket to her other arm and trudged on. What would she say to Ma?

If not for Abe she'd pick up her skirts and dash back to Ashtabula. She halted at the edge of the clearing. Goldenrod and purple asters bloomed along the trace, and she could hear the honeybees pollinating the flowers. Crickets filled the fall-like afternoon with their song. Matty stared at the cabin.

Underneath a tree sat her mother. Her mother's hands were slowly stripping leaves from the stalks of herbs. She paused after a few stalks to rest.

Ma was gaunt, and her shoulders were even more stooped. She never looked up from her task, but only coughed now and then, while placing both hands on her chest.

Matty felt her palms grow clammy, and her stomach snarled in fear. Was Ma so sick that she'd die? And where was Teddy? Maybe he had died while she was gone! She'd never forgive herself if she couldn't see her baby brother one more time.

She made her feet move forward until she stood in front of Ma. She could feel Ma's eyes move upward, scanning her from feet to face. Matty began to twist one of her bonnet strings, as they stared at each other.

Matty licked her lips. "I worked as a penman on a boat, Ma!" she blurted. "Mr. Spencer found me the job so I could earn my passage home."

Ma brushed a strand of hair from her face. Her hands were pale, and the raised veins made her hands look like corduroy. Never could Matty remember her mother having white hands.

"Abe told me that's where you had gone," her mother said. "Gone East to that school."

Matty lifted her chin. Same old Ma. "I had to go, Ma. I had to go somehow."

"So you ran away . . ." her mother's voice trailed off, and her eyes gazed over at the woods. "But you came back," she murmured.

"Abe wrote. He asked me to come home. He said he needed me." Matty bit her lip. Abe, she was doing this for Abe. And there was no reason to cower. She had stood up to those boys, hadn't she? She straightened her shoulders. "I'm home to help until you're feeling fit, then I'll be leaving. Mr. Spencer offered me an apprenticeship at his business college." And I'll be troubling you no further, she wanted to add, just allow me to see Teddy.

Her mother's hands trembled. "I see," she whispered.

Matty began to walk toward the cabin door, but one of her mother's hands caught her arm. Her mother's touch felt like a child's hand, it was so light. Matty looked down at the hand and then to her mother's face. Her mother's lips quivered, and there were tears at the edges of her eyes. Matty held her breath.

Ma cry? Matty stared at the hand. Slowly Ma's hand moved down Matty's arm and grasped Matty's own hand. Matty let out her breath and squeezed Ma's hand. It was cold and papery. Matty swallowed, placed her other hand over Ma's, and held it until Ma's hand warmed.

"It will be good to see everyone," Matty said, and she knew that she meant it. The snarl of fear had loosened itself. "Where's Teddy?" Matty asked. She sniffed, and raising one of her hands, she wiped tears from the corner of her eyes.

"Napping. He's asked for you repeatedly," Ma said. She still held Matty's hand. She squeezed it one more time. "Why don't you wake him?"

Matty tiptoed into the cabin. Teddy was curled up on Ma's bed. One fist held a corner of the quilt that covered him. Matty resisted the urge to scoop him up. He looked frail and thin.

She set her basket on the table and looked about the cabin. There were more cobwebs than when she left, and no one had cleaned the hearth for weeks. She sighed. Such a gloomy place compared to the Spencers' home. Log cabins just seem to attract dirt. But the seminary had been built from logs, and it was airy and light. What had made it and the Spencer home seem so cheerful?

Matty closed her eyes and saw the cherry dining room table graced by a bouquet. The china shone on the sideboard, and the air was fragrant with honeysuckle. She could almost hear Mrs. Spencer singing in the kitchen. She cracked open her eyes a bit. No china and no flowers on this table, only the crumbs of the last meal. She frowned. What would this cabin look like with flowers and china?

She closed her eyes again and tried to envision gleaming log walls with fresh chinking and muslin curtains at the window. There should be a well-scrubbed table and upon it a vase of asters and a steaming cup of tea.

Matty fumbled in her basket. She brought out the teacup Mrs. Spencer had given her. She wiped a place on the cupboard for it and set it there. A weak ray of sunshine lighted the pink flowers on the cup.

If she washed the windows, the cup would shine even more. Matty turned around. If she worked hard, the room could look like the one in her mind. She could battle the gloom, just like she had stood up to those boys. She could make the cabin feel like the Spencers' home. She remembered how Ma's hand had warmed at her touch. She would just have to keep the vision in her head of how this home could be. Maybe it was like making letters. First you had to see something in your mind before you could make it.

Teddy stirred and stretched. His eyes opened and widened. "Matty," he squealed. He sat up and held out his arms.

Matty ran to him and squeezed him. He clung to her while she rocked him back and forth. She nuzzled her face in his soft hair. "Back," Teddy said. "Come back."

Matty brushed away tears. "Back to you, Teddy. Back home. And for Ma, too, I reckon.

"Would you like to help me pick flowers for the table?" Matty asked, and squeezed him again.

Teddy nodded his head. "Flowers, pick."

Matty pulled his little romper on. Swinging Teddy on to her hip, she felt her pebble press against her leg. Thank goodness she hadn't thrown it into Lake Erie! She'd use it to weight papers on her table, and tonight she'd write Phineas with her new pen.

"Outside?" Teddy asked.

"Outside," Matty answered. "To those most perfect shapes." Together they would gather flowers for the cabin, and she would find a pebble for Teddy's pocket.

AUTHOR'S NOTE

There really was a man who once practiced penmanship on the sides of a ship, and he even used his own blood to pen a drawing. His name was Platt Rogers Spencer, the father of American penmanship. From 1853 to 1863, Mr. Spencer taught at his Jericho Log Cabin Seminary just outside of Geneva, Ohio, on Jericho Road.

Matty and Phineas are not real people, but they represent the hundreds of students who gathered at Mr. Spencer's school and then taught his system of penmanship throughout our country. The other characters, even the rascally twins, and most of the events of the story are true and based on research.

Spencerian Script became the most widely taught system of handwriting in America, and Mr. Spencer's workbook sold more than one million copies before his death in 1864. After his death the art of handwriting flourished during a time when good penmanship was a coveted skill.

Besides teaching his script, Mr. Spencer was known as an abolitionist, a poet, and a leader in the temperance movement. Mr. Spencer always credited Persis's prayerful support as the key to his own recovery from alcohol.

President Garfield respected Mr. Spencer, and he summarized the sentiments of others by saying, "To the thousands of young men and women who enjoyed the benefits of his brilliant instructions . . . the memory of his life will remain a perpetual benediction." Mr. Spencer's script is still taught today in calligraphy classes where America's penmanship legacy lives on.

BIBLIOGRAPHY

Ashtabula County Historical Society. *1889 History of Ashtabula County, Ohio, with Illustration and Biographical Sketches of Its Pioneers and Most Prominent Men.* Philadelphia: Williams Brothers, 1898.

Geneva Public Library (Geneva, Ohio). Spencerian Collection, 1989.

Knowles and Maxim. *Golden Gems of Penmanship and Self-Instructor.* Pittsfield, Mass., Knowles and Maxim. 1884.

Penman's Art Journal. March 1896. New York, N.Y.

Spencer, Harvey, and Brothers. *Spencer Brothers' Copy-books.* 2nd edition. New York: American Book Co., 1891.

Spencer, H. C. *Spencerian Key to Practical Penmanship.* New York: Phinney, Blakeman & Co., 1867.

"Spencerian Writing System." *The Sunday Times.* August 14, 1949. Erie, Penn.

"Spencer's Log Seminary." *Geneva Free Press.* February 23, 1891. Geneva, Ohio.

Sugarman, Joan. *The Spencerian Heritage: Reawakening the Tradition of Good Penmanship.* Cleveland: Dyke College, 1976.

Sull, Michael. *Spencerian Script and Ornamental Penmanship.* Prairie Village, Kan.: The Lettering Design Group, 1989.

And numerous hours spent with Michael Sull for instruction and discussion on America's penmanship history.